THE MURDERS AT IMPASSE LOUVAIN

THE MURDERS AT IMPASSE LOUVAIN

A NOVEL

by

RICHARD GRAYSON

ST. MARTIN'S PRESS NEW YORK

c. 1

M

Library of Congress Cataloging in Publication Data

— — — —

The murders at Impasse Louvain.

I.   Title.
PZ4.G866Mu   1979   [PR6057.R55]   823'.9'14   79-5038
ISBN 0-312-55343-9

BL

JAN 4   1980

THE MURDERS AT IMPASSE LOUVAIN

I

GAUTIER LAY WITH his eyes closed, awake, but unwilling completely to surrender the luxury of sleep. He could hear his wife, Suzanne, moving in the kitchen but that part of the bed where she had been lying beside him was still warm, so she could not have been up for long. He had at least ten minutes surely before the smell of coffee would come drifting into the bedroom and he would need to go and join her for breakfast.

His wish to linger on in bed had nothing to do with indolence. Gautier was not a lazy man. For six days a week he would rise without prompting soon after six, giving himself time to walk to headquarters and still arrive there well before most of his colleagues. Even on those weekdays when he was not on duty, he would be out of bed before most people in Paris were leaving for work.

Sundays were different. The moment of waking on Sunday morning was a time of different sensuous pleasures, each of which had to be savoured slowly: warmth, the comfort of bed, the relaxation of separate muscles, the smell of coffee and fresh bread and above all the silence.

Although he had lived in the country as a boy, the silence and stillness of Paris early on Sunday morning still astonished Gautier. No sound of horses or cartwheels came from the street outside, nor the shouts of tradesmen offering their produce to cooks and housewives. On weekdays, even though their apartment was on the fourth floor, the voices of the women, arguing about prices, came echoing up, bouncing off the walls of the buildings in the narrow street, seeming louder than life. On Sundays all was still even in the apartment building; no sound of children's footsteps running down the stairs, no banging of pots and pans by women half-awake, no men's voices raised in anger. Men, Gautier had noticed, seldom beat their wives on Sundays.

His enjoyment of these sensations of early morning was sharpened by an unconscious anticipation of other small pleasures to come as Sunday unfurled itself. After breakfast, at Mass, the precise cadences of the Latin responses appealed to his senses even more than the flickering of tall candles and the smell of incense. Later there would be other pleasures: the mild shock to the palate of the first aperitif, the smell of gigot cooked in a subtle blend of herbs, drowsiness after three glasses of red wine and one of very old Calvados, the rumbling laugh of his father-in-law.

They lunched every Sunday with Suzanne's parents, her sister and her sister's husband. The old man had made a bit of money. Starting with a china shop up in Bagnolet, he had expanded and then switched to wholesale selling. Now he had a business supplying china and glass to many of the thousands of cafés and restaurants in Paris. He was not exactly a Chauchard, the millionaire owner of the Louvre department store, nor a Camille Grout, the miller who entertained royalty in his house on Avenue du Bois, but he had enough to take his children and their husbands out to a substantial lunch every Sunday. In winter they would eat at one of the better family restaurants on the Left Bank, but as soon as the weather grew warm enough, they would make an expedition out of Paris and lunch on the banks of the Seine.

Gautier was thinking about the lunch to come, savouring in his imagination the food and the wine and the delicious sense of indolence which went with them, when he heard a knock at the door of the apartment. Suzanne answered it and presently she called out to him.

'What is it?' he shouted back.

'A man from the fifteenth arrondissement with a message.'

Swearing sadly to himself, he pulled on a pair of trousers and went barefoot to the hallway. The uniformed policeman who stood there talking to Suzanne had the lean, dark features of the Midi or perhaps Corsica. Gautier did not recognize him but more than two years had passed since he had been transferred from the commissariat of the fifteenth arrondissement to the headquarters of the Sûreté.

'Well?' he asked the man.

'There have been two deaths in Impasse Louvain, Inspector. Looks like murder.'

'So?'

'The commissaire telephoned the Sûreté. He was told to ask you to go to the house and take charge.'

'But I'm not even on duty today!'

'I understand the instructions came from the director himself.'

'Are you telling me that the Director of the Sûreté has been bothered with this? On a Sunday morning?'

'I wouldn't know about that, Inspector.'

After the man had left to return to the commissariat, Gautier dressed. Suzanne found him a clean shirt, then went to pour his coffee. Most wives would have protested or sulked but she never complained when one of the few days they could spend together was disrupted or he was pulled out of bed by some emergency. At times Gautier felt that she was almost too patient, too philosophic. If he had been jealous by disposition, he might have wondered whether she had a lover in the background.

Impasse Louvain was a short cul-de-sac off Rue de Vaugirard, less than ten minutes walk from his home. On his way there Gautier found himself wondering why the name of the street seemed to stir some vague recollection from the past. He could remember passing the corner where it joined Rue de Vaugirard often enough, but was certain that he had never actually entered the cul-de-sac.

The house to which he had been directed was surrounded by a six-foot wall and a policeman in uniform was standing outside the gate. Apart from this one man the street was empty which meant that the murders—if they were murders—could only have been reported a short time ago. Even on Sundays it did not take long in Paris for curious spectators to gather. Gautier knew the policeman at the gate and stopped to exchange a few words with him.

'Who's inside?' He nodded towards the house.

'Commissaire Druot and one of my colleagues.'

'Anyone else?'

'A neighbour who reported the deaths and the family doctor.

7

Madame Hassler is in a bad way. It was her husband and her mother who were murdered, you know.'

'Hassler? Not Josephine Hassler?'

'Yes, Inspector.'

Gautier realized then why the name Impasse Louvain had tugged at his memory. Not many years previously Josephine Hassler had achieved a spectacular notoriety in Paris. She was the wife of an artist, Félix Hassler, who in spite of the mediocrity of his work, had been commissioned by several wealthy and influential men to paint their portraits. Madame Hassler had built up a modest salon in her house in Impasse Louvain, but it was not in her own drawing-room that her name became linked with scandal but in a place no less exalted than the Elysée Palace.

The late President of France had died suddenly one evening, according to the medical bulletins of an apoplectic fit. Then members of his staff made it known that Josephine Hassler had been at the palace late in the afternoon of his death, alone with the president in his private apartments. Sentries had seen her leaving, hurriedly and by the main entrance instead of by the side door which she normally used, for she was a regular visitor and supposed to be helping the president to write his memoirs. A servant found a woman's corset stuffed into a drawer of the president's desk.

A rumour was soon circling Paris that the president's secretary, hearing a woman's screams, had broken down the locked door of his study and found him dying, his hands still clutching the hair of his naked mistress. Newspapers did not hesitate to print the story, not naming the woman, but stating that she was the wife of a painter whose surname began with the initial 'H'. They said too that the president had been taking aphrodisiacs and indulging in sexual pastimes too freely for a man of his age. Government ministers were accused of deliberately concealing the truth from the public and the scandal was a long time dying.

Remembering this, Gautier understood why the Director of the Sûreté had been informed of the deaths at the house in Impasse Louvain. This was going to be a case that needed careful handling.

When he passed through the gate in the wall, he found that the house was surrounded by a small garden and a path led round the side, presumably to a servants' entrance. The front entrance was by way of a verandah and he noticed that the second of the upper floors of the house had unusually large windows which, he guessed, must belong to the painter's studio.

The front door was not locked and in the drawing-room beyond the verandah Druot, his former boss in the fifteenth arrondissement, was talking to a plump little man with a grey beard. The drawing-room was all of 60 feet long and about half as broad. At one end there was an enormous chimney piece of carved wood which was flanked on each side by glass-fronted cabinets filled with china and silver. One wall was hung with a Gobelin tapestry depicting the story of Judith and the room also housed a small organ and a grand piano and a mass of potted palms and flowers.

When Druot saw Gautier he said:

'Ah, Inspector! This is Monsieur Gide who lives in the house opposite. It was he who reported the murders.'

'You have established that they were murders?'

'Hassler was strangled. The doctor isn't certain about the old lady, but he believes she was asphyxiated when she swallowed her dentures. On the other hand he doesn't rule out the possibility of a heart attack.'

'And where is Madame Hassler?'

'She's with the doctor now, suffering from shock. It appears that the gang who broke in to rob the house last night left her bound and gagged in her bed for more than six hours.'

'Was there no one else in the house? The Hasslers have a daughter, I seem to remember.'

'She has been staying in their house outside Paris for the past few days.'

'And servants?'

'The cook is also staying in the country house. There is a man-servant as well who was sleeping in the attic room and who says he heard nothing. It was he who found Madame Hassler this morning.'

The neighbour Gide added: 'I was passing in the lane outside when I heard him shouting for help from a first-floor window.'

He was a law-abiding fellow, Gautier decided, of good bourgeois upbringing and probably married to a domineering wife.

'Have you taken any statements?' Gautier asked Druot.

'No, I've left that to you.' The commissaire was clearly pleased to be passing on this responsibility. Presumably he too had plans for his Sunday. 'The director wants you to take charge and he has promised to look in himself later.'

'Then I had better go upstairs and take a look at the bodies.'

'Will it be all right if I go now?' Gide asked. 'My family will be wondering what has become of me.'

'Certainly, Monsieur, but I may wish to ask you some questions later in the day.'

Gautier shook hands with him and with Druot and watched the two men leave before he went upstairs. A second uniformed police-man standing at the head of the stairs explained the geography of the house to him. On the first floor there were three bedrooms, one each for Félix Hassler and his wife who no longer shared a bed and a smaller room for their daughter Marguerite. Josephine had evidently spent the previous night in this latter bedroom, having given up her own room, which was a good deal larger, to her elderly mother. A small boudoir separated the bedrooms of the two women and at the end of the corridor, next to Hassler's room, there was a bathroom.

Hassler's body, covered now by a blanket, was still lying where it had been found in the doorway between his bedroom and the bathroom. Lifting the blanket, Gautier saw a man of about 60 with a bullet-shaped head and grizzled hair, cropped short. He was wearing a long nightshirt and lay with his legs bent under his thighs as though he had died in a kneeling position and had then slumped over to one side. His face was distorted in the grimace of strangulation and a rope was knotted round his neck. His ankles and wrists were bound with cord.

Gautier noticed that the rope did not appear to be biting into the throat of the dead man. Curious, he took hold of it between one thumb and forefinger and found he could slide the loop quite easily up and down Hassler's neck. He found a slight discolour-ation of the flesh under the place where the rope had been, but it had left no mark to speak of and certainly not the deep weal that one would have expected.

He passed through the bathroom and into the bedroom on the other side of the corridor. The body of an old woman who must have been Josephine Hassler's mother, lay on the bed, arms folded across the breast in an attitude that would have seemed peaceful had it not been for the colour of the face and the rigid stare of death in the eyes. A piece of cottonwool had been stuffed into her mouth and more lay on the pillow by her head. Her ankles were also bound.

The policeman stood guard on the landing outside the door of the third bedroom and Gautier asked him:

'Is the doctor still with Madame Hassler?'

'Yes, Inspector.'

'And where is the manservant?'

'I last saw him downstairs in the kitchen at the back of the house.'

'What do they call him?'

'Mansard. Remy Mansard.'

Gautier went downstairs. Mansard was slim and fair-haired, with that air of innocence which is sometimes taken for good looks but which could equally be a sign of stupidity. He was wearing beige trousers and a green-and-gold-striped waistcoat and was pretending, not very convincingly, to polish a basket of household silver. When Gautier came into the kitchen he stood up quickly.

'Sit down,' Gautier said and taking a chair he sat down opposite Mansard across the table. 'You're the one who shouted for help out of the window this morning?'

'Yes, Sir.'

'Then tell me exactly what happened.'

The manservant's narration of the morning's events, disjointed and repetitive, would have been difficult enough to follow even without his heavy accent, almost a patois, which Gautier recognized as coming from Normandy. The essential facts were that Mansard had woken at six o'clock. On his way downstairs to light the kitchen stove, a task he was expected to carry out when the cook was away, he heard a muffled cry from the room of the Hasslers' daughter. Inside he had found the mistress of the house bound to the bed, distraught and talking feverishly about a gang of robbers with revolvers who had broken into her room at midnight and threatened her. Her wrists had been bound to the head of the bed and her ankles to the bedrail at the bottom. One end of the rope tying her wrists was also knotted round her neck.

Mansard had undone the knots at her wrists and she had then told him to go and get help. So he had gone first to Hassler's room thinking to wake his master and found Hassler's body. Remembering that Madame Hassler's mother had also been sleeping in the house, he had then tried the remaining bedroom and discovered her dead body as well. Horrified he had rushed to the nearest window, thrown it open and shouted for help. The neighbour Monsieur Gide had been passing in the lane outside and it was he who had telephoned for the police.

When Mansard had finished, Gautier asked him: 'Tell me, was your mistress gagged when you found her?'

'Not when I went into her room, but she had been gagged and had managed just at that moment to spit the cottonwool out. I noticed that a large lump of it was lying on the pillow beside her head.'

'This rope round her neck. Do you think the thieves had meant to strangle her like your master?'

'Oh no, Monsieur! It was really knotted quite loosely. And the ropes round her wrists and ankles were not at all tightly knotted. I remember thinking as I undid them that with a little effort she might have been able to free herself.'

Leaving him with the cutlery to clean, Gautier went back to the drawing-room and found the telephone. Telephones were still rare in Paris but his wife's parents had recently treated themselves to the luxury of one. He put a call through to them, explained that he had been called out on duty, that there was no chance at all of his being able to join the family for lunch and that they should warn Suzanne it might well be late that night before he returned home. As he was finishing the call he saw Courtrand, the Director of the Sûreté, coming into the house through the verandah.

'This is a nasty business, Gautier,' the director said. 'How are your enquiries progressing?'

'I've looked at the two bodies and I've questioned the manservant.'

'And Madame Hassler?'

'She's upstairs in her room with the family doctor. I thought I should wait until you arrived before taking her statement.'

'Quite right!' Courtrand nodded approvingly. He was a man

who attached great importance to procedure and protocol. 'But in any case I gather it's a straightforward case of murder by armed intruders.'

'Not entirely straightforward, Monsieur le Directeur.'

'Why did you say that?'

'Hassler was strangled, but not by the rope around his neck. That was quite clearly placed there after he was dead. Now why should anyone want to do that?'

II

GAUTIER'S ROOM IN the headquarters of the Sûreté, like the offices in most French government departments, was dismal. It could not even be said in defence of the room that it was functional and one felt that those who had designed and furnished it had used all their ingenuity to make it as bleak and cheerless as possible, in the belief that policemen should be out catching criminals and not wasting their time in office work. Even the last sunlight of the evening, slanting through the branches of a tree outside, instead of softening the harsh outlines of the drab furniture and the cold walls, only made them seem more gloomy. Sometimes Gautier thought of the room as a mortuary, a repository not of dead bodies but of ancient crimes, forgotten but still festering.

On the desk in front of him lay a copy of the statement which Josephine Hassler had made to Courtrand that morning in his presence. He had compiled it from notes he had taken when Courtrand had questioned Madame Hassler and it had been type-written by a clerk on one of the cumbersome new machines which the Department had only recently acquired. Then he had taken the finished statement back to Impasse Louvain so that Madame Hassler might sign it. Courtrand, who had gone off just before lunch to resume his interrupted Sunday, would expect to have the statement on his desk next morning for his signature before it was admitted into the dossier which they would now start building up on the case. That was the system and in his more cynical moods Gautier wondered whether it might not be better if the Sûreté were entirely staffed by clerks and scribes.

Preparing the statement had not been easy because Josephine Hassler, although she had kept protesting that she was exhausted and on the verge of a breakdown, had talked volubly, almost endlessly. Courtrand had scarcely needed to put questions to her. Her story of the events of the previous night and of what had led up to them, long and rambling, punctuated with irrelevancies and digressions, left out no fact that could possibly have been of any value to the police. Reading the statement now, Gautier was rather proud of the editing job he had done.

STATEMENT ON OATH

This Sunday, 1 June, we Gustave Courtrand, Commander of the Légion d'Honneur, Director-General of the Sûreté, heard on oath Josephine Hassler who declared:

'I had been staying in our country home at Bellevue with my daughter, Marguerite, and I came up to Paris yesterday (Saturday), to meet my mother who was coming to spend a few days with us. My husband had been in Paris while we were away as he had two important commissions to finish, but he was going to come down to Bellevue as well over the weekend and stay until Monday at least. My mother arrived at Gare St Lazare at mid-day and we did some shopping during the afternoon, intending to take the train to Bellevue early in the evening. However by the end of the afternoon, my mother seemed very tired and her legs, which had been troubling her for some months, grew more and more painful. So I decided it would be unwise to travel and that we should spend the night in Paris to enable her to rest. We had only one servant in the house as our cook, Françoise, was in Bellevue too, nor had we much food. Remy made us a light meal of pâté and lobster and we dined early at about seven, I think it was. We were all tired, so we decided to go to bed soon after nine. To make my mother as comfortable as possible, I decided she should sleep in my room, which is the largest bedroom, and I slept in my daughter's tiny bed. I was sleeping soundly when quite suddenly I awoke. I felt something covering my face – later I saw it was a towel – and that frightened me. In a panic I pulled it away and saw that there was a light in the room. Two men and a woman were standing round the bed.

The woman said to me in a threatening voice: "Tell us where your parents keep their money and their jewels." She was holding a revolver pointed at my temple. I was terrified and began to tremble. She repeated her question about the money and I pointed to the door which led into the boudoir. One of the men came forward and began tying my wrists and ankles to the bed. I noticed that all three of them were wearing long, black robes; long and straight, cut all in one piece and with wide sleeves. They were not unlike the robes that priests wear, but black and made from some heavy, woollen material. One of the men was holding a lantern. The woman held my arm tightly and was still aiming the revolver at my head. "Please don't kill me," I begged her.

After binding my ankles and wrists to the bed, the man put a rope round my neck and then stuffed some cottonwool into my mouth. Finally they again covered my face with the towel. I heard the woman ask: "Why are we wasting time?" She was very ugly with black, frizzy hair, a wicked mouth and black circles painted round her eyes. She said "Why don't we finish her off?" One of the men replied: "No, leave the little one alone." I realized then that they had mistaken me for my daughter. You see, I was sleeping in her bed. Presently I heard them leaving the room. I couldn't scream for help because of the gag they had put in my mouth and when I tried to move, the rope around my neck tightened, strangling me. Sheer terror must have made me dizzy because I was certain I was going to die. Then I suppose I fainted and the next thing I knew it was morning. At first when I woke I was still too frightened to move but after a struggle I managed to spit the gag out of my mouth. I heard someone passing in the corridor outside the room and guessing that it must be the manservant, Remy, I called out to him. He came, undid the ropes round my wrists and then went for help. It was not until Monsieur Gide arrived that I learned that both my mother and my husband had been murdered.'

I then asked Madame Hassler if she knew what time in the night she had been attacked and she declared:

'It was close to midnight when I awoke and found the robbers in my room. I know that because I heard the clock of the church chiming twelve.'

When I asked Madame Hassler what had been stolen from the house she stated:

'They took three rings and 6,000 francs in banknotes which I had placed on the dressing-table in the room. As far as I know they took nothing else, but I have not had time to check if any of my mother's and husband's possessions are missing. All our silver was concealed in a hiding place in the dining-room and that has not been touched.'

Finally when I asked Madame Hassler if she knew how the intruders could have got into the house she stated:

'I have no idea, unless of course they broke in. My husband locked the front door of the house before we went upstairs. The back door was the responsibility of the servants and I suppose Remy must have locked that as usual.'

Gautier put the statement down on the desk in front of him, leant back in his chair and looked at the darkening sky outside. It was not Josephine Hassler's story, bizarre and improbable though it must seem, that was bothering him. After a few years of service in the police, his capacity for astonishment had dwindled almost completely away.

He was thinking not of the statement nor of Josephine Hassler, but of the Director of the Sûreté. Everyone said that Courtrand's had been a political appointment and it was true that he possessed few of the qualifications that would be expected in his post. Even so, Gautier had always found him shrewd and tough. His behaviour at Impasse Louvain that morning was for that reason all the more difficult to explain.

He had treated Josephine Hassler with a courtesy and consideration that had bordered on subservience. Gautier had seemed to sense, although Courtrand had addressed her in formal terms throughout, an understanding between him and the woman, not strong enough to be called intimacy, but an understanding nevertheless. On the other hand he supposed it might merely have been

Courtrand's instinctive response to an attractive woman. In spite of her 40-odd years, Madame Hassler was still beautiful, with an oval face, regular features and dark eyes which she knew how to use to good effect. She had received the two of them in her daughter's bedroom, wearing a flowered negligee which showed off her throat and shoulders. Once when she had leaned forward, perhaps deliberately, the front of the garment had parted and Gautier had seen quite plainly through the diaphanous nightdress underneath, her breasts, ample but still firm.

When they had left her and were going downstairs from the bedroom, Courtrand had asked him: 'Well, what is your opinion, Gautier?'

'Of Madame Hassler's story?'

'Yes.'

'One has to recognize that she has a remarkable imagination.'

'What do you mean?'

'No one in their right mind would believe a tale like that, Monsieur.'

Courtrand looked at him sharply. 'Why not?'

'Men with beards wearing long black cloaks! Lanterns and pistols! And are we really supposed to believe that they would mistake Madame Hassler for a seventeen-year-old girl, well preserved though she certainly is? If they were robbers why did they leave behind Hassler's gold watch and wallet containing 8,000 francs which were lying on the table only a few feet from where he lay dead?'

'Once we have laid our hands on the intruders, no doubt we'll have the answers to those questions,' Courtrand said stiffly. 'With the excellent description that Madame Hassler has given us of them, it should not be too difficult to track them down.'

III

TWO MEN WIDELY different in appearance and temperament worked as assistants to Gautier in the Sûreté. Nordel was in his 30s, clever in a superficial way and ambitious. Surat was one of the old school, not far from retirement, painstaking, physically courageous and completely loyal.

In his office next morning, Gautier gave both men a brief summary of the 'Affair at Impasse Louvain', as it was already being called, and let them read the statement made by Josephine Hassler. He did not make the mistake as Courtrand had with him of asking them for their comments.

'We have to find these people who committed the two murders,' he told Nordel, 'and there is not much to go on except their disguises. Long black robes and false beards are not all that common and could, with any luck, be traced. The robes which Madame Hassler described sound to me very much like those which Jewish priests wear, so start checking with every synagogue to see if any have been stolen. On the other hand they could just be costumes. Get some men to help you and visit all theatrical costumiers as well.'

Nordel looked at him incredulously. 'Are we to believe Madame Hassler's story?'

'The director insists that we find these people at all costs,' Gautier replied, evading the question as best he could.

After Nordel had left the room he gave Surat his instructions. He told him to find out everything he could about Josephine Hassler, her background, her family, her upbringing, how and in what circumstances she had come to marry a man twenty years older than herself, the sort of fees that Félix Hassler commanded as a portrait painter, the style in which they lived. A few enquiries among the tradesmen from whom the cook of the house made her daily purchases would give a fair indication of the household budget. He remembered that in the 15th arrondissement the local police had standing instructions to keep an eye on number 8, Impasse Louvain, as a house frequented by 'hautes personalités'. Surat was to discover as discreetly as possible, the names of these VIPs and establish whether they were regular visitors at Madame Hassler's salon.

'What about that affair at the Elysée Palace?' Surat asked.

'No, leave that alone. We had better not go raking around in that particular dung-heap; for the time being anyway.' Gautier looked at Surat steadily for a moment before adding: 'And your report must be confidential to me. You and I can decide later how much of it will go into the official dossier.'

Surat left the room looking pleased. He was not too old or too cynical to find pleasure in knowing that he was being specially trusted. Probably he also realized that Nordel would not have been given the same assignment.

Gautier took a copy of Madame Hassler's statement down to the director's office and left it with the director's personal assistant. Courtrand worked gentleman's hours and was seldom at his desk before ten.

Outside the morning sun had put a sheen on the waters of the Seine and the sky was clear, but the air was soft and moist, suggesting rain later in the day. The driver of a fiacre which stood waiting on the opposite side of the street, was shouting jovially to a bouquiniste who had just opened up his second-hand book stall on the quay overlooking the river. A coupé drawn by two fine white horses passed at a brisk pace, heading westward. Gautier caught a glimpse of a florid man in evening dress slumped against the cushions inside, his face frozen in the vacuous grimace of drunken sleep; a clubman, no doubt, returning home after a night of debauchery.

Enjoying the exercise, Gautier walked along by the river, crossed to the Left Bank by Pont St Michel and boarded an omnibus in Boulevard St Germain, testing his agility by climbing the precarious stairs that led to the upper deck as the horses moved off at a trot. Drivers of omnibuses, he had noticed, seemed to take a perverse delight in endangering the lives not only of their passengers but of any pedestrians who might be rash enough to step anywhere near the path of the flying hooves and cumbersome wheels.

A small crowd had already assembled outside the front gate of number 8, Impasse Louvain. Most were inquisitive spectators but among them half-a-dozen journalists had been trying to persuade the policeman at the gate to let them pass.

One of the journalists, recognizing Gautier, called out: 'What about it, Inspector? Can't we get in to interview Madame Hassler?'

'I'll ask her if she'll see you.'

He made his way round to the back door of the house and found it open. In the kitchen the manservant, Mansard, was seated at a table, smoking a cigar and turning over the pages of a newspaper. His face wore a frown of concentration as he read aloud, spelling out the words. When he saw Gautier come in, he flushed and tried to hide the cigar.

'That's all right,' Gautier remarked. 'We don't mind if you take cigars from journalists or even a few francs, just so long as you don't start making up any fancy tales for them to print.'

'No, Sir, of course I wouldn't.'

'In the meantime I have a question or two for you to answer. For a start what time did you go to bed on Saturday night?'

'At about half-past-nine. After the master and mistress and Madame Pinock had gone upstairs, I finished cleaning up and then went to my room.'

'And you heard nothing at all during the night?'

'Nothing, Sir. But then my room and the cook's are in the attic and there's the master's studio between us and the first floor where the family sleeps. Also I am a very heavy sleeper.'

'But you're sure Monsieur and Madame Hassler and the old lady were already in their rooms when you went up.'

'Oh, yes. You see, on my way to bed I took them the grog.'

'Grog?'

'The mistress decided that they would all take a grog before going to sleep. So I took up a tray with glasses, a jug of hot water, the rum and a bowl of sugar.'

'Did the Hasslers often drink grog at night?'

'Very seldom. The master would sometimes take one, but Madame Hassler always said she hated the smell of rum. That night was the first time I ever heard her ask for a grog.'

'And where did you take the tray?'

'To mademoiselle's bedroom. The mistress was to sleep there, you see. She told me she would mix the grog and take it into the others.'

'I see. And did you bring the tray and the glasses downstairs yesterday morning?'

'No, Sir. With so much happening and the shock of finding the master and the old lady dead, I forgot. Then after you and the other policemen arrived, I was told not to touch anything in the rooms where the bodies were found or in the boudoir.'

As he questioned Mansard, Gautier was watching him. The manservant seemed ill-at-ease, more so than timidity or a country youth's fear of the police would explain. From time to time he looked at Gautier, quick anxious glances which suggested that he might be holding back some information.

'What did you tell the journalists?' Gautier asked him suddenly.

'Tell them, Monsieur? I don't know what you mean.'

'Come on, let's have it! It will all be in the papers tomorrow and you can expect trouble if we find out you've been concealing information.'

Mansard hesitated. 'I know nothing about the murders.'

'Did you lock the back door last night before you went to bed?'

'Yes, Monsieur.'

'But the neighbour Gide says he found it open.'

'Then someone else must have opened it.'

'Who?'

Again Mansard hesitated before he said sullenly: 'I don't know, but I do know someone came to the house after I came upstairs.'

'Then you did hear something?'

'No, but when I went to my room I read for a time. Madame Hassler doesn't like it, because she doesn't want to waste candles.' He paused for a moment and then, as though to justify his disobedience said petulantly: 'Mean old goat! Anyway, when eventually I blew out the candle I got out of bed to pull back the curtains and let in the moonlight. That was when I saw him.'

'Who? The man who came to the house?'

'No. The man who was standing in the lane outside. He's always there waiting every time a certain person comes to the house and stays there until the caller leaves. Must be a servant I suppose, or perhaps a bodyguard.'

'And who is the person he waits for?'

'I can't say, for I've never actually seen him, but he must be someone important.'

'And that night you didn't actually see anyone come into the house?'

'No, but he was there all right. The same man as always. You can count on that.'

The man could be lying, Gautier reflected. He might have invented the story because journalists were pestering him or simply to draw attention to himself. Mansard appeared honest enough, but Gautier knew from experience that in the atmosphere of nervous excitement which always surrounded violent death, ordinary, predictable people often did or said extraordinary, unpredictable things.

'This fellow you saw in the street outside the house; couldn't he have been a look-out for the intruders who Madame Hassler says tied her up?'

The manservant laughed. 'Intruders my arse! Anyway she says they didn't break in until around midnight, and when I saw this man it couldn't have been much after ten.'

His manner irritated Gautier, perhaps because the man was voicing a suspicion which he shared, but one which he had been forced to keep to himself because Courtrand refused to entertain it. He said to Mansard harshly: 'Who is saying that they broke in? There was no sign of a forcible entry. We believe they must have had an accomplice in the house.'

He left the manservant looking confused and shaken by the innuendo and went through the door which separated the kitchen from the rest of the house. His intention was to go upstairs to the bedrooms, but as he was passing the door to the drawing-room, he heard the voice of Josephine Hassler. Thinking that he should at least let her know that he was in the house, he went in and found

23

Courtrand was also there. The two of them were sitting on a sofa, not too far apart, arguing so it seemed and heatedly.

When they saw it was Gautier coming in, Madame Hassler broke off what she was saying in mid-sentence. Courtrand merely looked at his watch and remarked: 'Ah, there you are, Inspector! I wondered when you would get here.'

Tricky little swine! Gautier thought, but at the same time he could not help but admire the man's sang-froid and the skill with which he had put his subordinate on the defensive.

'I've been having a few words with the manservant, Sir,' he said.

'Good! And I'm glad you have arrived because I think we should ask Madame Hassler to check and make absolutely sure how much of her property was stolen. Once we have a list we can start trying to trace the stolen pieces and that may help lead us to the murderers.' He turned and looked at Josephine Hassler. 'Would you be so kind as to assist us, Madame?'

'Willingly, Monsieur le Directeur.'

The three of them went upstairs. After taking Madame Hassler's statement the previous day, Courtrand and Gautier had made a preliminary search of the three bedrooms on the first floor as well as the boudoir. They had found nothing that would help them identify the intruders. Each of the rooms had been in disarray, as though they had been hastily, but not too thoroughly searched. Cupboard doors had been left open, drawers pulled out. In the bedroom where the old lady had been found dead and also in the daughter's bedroom, they had found quantities of cottonwool lying on and around the beds, presumably the same cottonwool that had been used to gag the women. Afterwards, to conform with police procedure, once the bodies of Félix Hassler and his mother-in-law had been taken away for autopsy, the rooms in which they had been found dead had been locked and police seals fixed across the doors. The Director of the Sûreté had the authority to break these seals, but only in the presence of an official witness.

As they climbed the stairs, Josephine Hassler walked slowly and unsteadily, holding on to the banister rail. Courtrand took her arm solicitously. When they reached the landing, she stopped and looked at Gautier.

'Forgive me, Inspector, but this has been a very great strain for me. My doctor says I must have been very near death that night and that it is only my exceptional strength and courage that permit me to keep going.'

'We will be as quick and as gentle as possible, Madame,' Courtrand promised her.

After removing the seals on the door, they went first into Félix Hassler's room. Apart from the body, nothing had been moved by the police. Hassler's gold watch and chain and his wallet still lay on the bedside table, together with a bunch of keys, a handkerchief that was slightly soiled with paint stains and a card case containing his visiting cards. Beside them stood a cheap alarm clock which had stopped, presumably because it had not been wound for two days. Gautier noticed that the alarm had been set to ring at half-past-eleven.

'Please be kind enough to watch me as I examine the contents of this wallet,' Courtrand said to Josephine Hassler and then he added to Gautier: 'Make a list, Inspector, if you please.'

The wallet held 8,000 francs in notes, a sizeable sum at a time when a lavish dinner for four people, including wine, would cost no more than 100 and when no family of any standing would think of paying cash for any purchase. Beside the notes, they found in the wallet a small sepia tinted photograph of a young girl and a bill from a firm supplying artists' materials.

'My husband cashed a cheque at the bank on Friday,' Madame Hassler explained. 'We were not sure how long we would be staying at Bellevue.'

'And can you see anything missing from this room?' Courtrand asked her.

'No. But then perhaps when the thieves discovered they had killed my husband, they panicked and fled.'

As they were leaving the room, Gautier stooped and began examining the bedclothes of the still unmade bed. Pulling the blankets back he looked carefully at the bottom sheet. Courtrand asked him impatiently what he was doing. He explained that when he had seen Hassler's body the previous day, he had noticed a blue stain on the left foot. Before leaving the Sûreté that morning he had spoken to the doctor at the mortuary who had confirmed that the stain was blue ink.

'Well? What does that mean?'

'I also noticed a blue stain on the drawing-room carpet, as though a bottle of ink had been knocked over there.'

'You're right,' Madame Hassler told him. 'The intruders must have knocked over the ink-well which I had left out on the table. I found the mess yesterday and made Remy clean it up.'

'If that's true then Monsieur Hassler must have been killed in the drawing-room and his body brought up here afterwards.'

'Why not?' Courtrand asked, shrugging his shoulders. 'He may have heard a noise, gone downstairs and disturbed the robbers. That may be why he was killed.'

Gautier made no comment. There were other questions he would have liked to have asked. Why for example there was no trace of ink on either the stairs leading up from the ground floor nor anywhere in Hassler's room. Aware of Courtrand's mood of protectiveness towards the Hassler woman, however, he decided that the questions could wait.

The larger of the other two bedrooms was furnished in a style far more elegant than that of the master of the house and clearly at much greater cost. Its walls were covered in lime green silk and hung with several ornate mirrors as well as a large painting of an allegorical theme, with a goddess reclining in the nude surrounded by cherubs holding cornucopiae brimming over with fruit. In style the painting was recognizable as the work of one of the great fashionable artists of the time, men like Messonier, Boldini and Puvis de Chavannes, who were commissioned by government departments and by wealthy art patrons, but were known derisively as 'pompiers' by the Impressionists and other young artists struggling for recognition. A 'style imperiale' settee stood at one end of the room, draped casually, but suggestively it seemed to Gautier, with a fur rug. The dressing-table, the bedside table, the mantelpiece, every square centimetre of available surface, were covered with bibelots and bric-à-brac in the fashion of the day: porcelain figures of nymphs and shepherds, a box carved in sandal-wood, cut-glass bottles with jewelled stoppers, a primitive carving of a negro head in black wood, family photographs in silver frames, a replica of the Eiffel Tower produced to commemorate its official opening in 1889, medals issued to mark the death of different presidents, tiny vases containing dried flowers, a fossilized sea-horse, a china nest full of brightly-coloured glass eggs. The luxuriance of the furnishings and the fabrics and the room's sensual décor would have been more suited, it seemed to Gautier, to the bedroom of a high-class cocotte, a Liane de Pougy or Emilienne d'Alençon, than that of a bourgeois painter's wife.

Josephine Hassler went round the room, opening drawers, looking at the ornaments and then said finally: 'I can see nothing missing.'

'Didn't your mother have any jewelry?'

'Yes, but she left most of it at home. All she was wearing when I met her at St Lazare was a pearl brooch and a wedding ring.'

'And they are both missing?'

'Yes, they're not here.'

The three of them passed into the next room which served as a boudoir and sewing-room and also contained a bureau, where Madame Hassler wrote letters and did the household accounts. Like the drawing-room and Madame Hassler's bedroom, it was full of bric-à-brac and standing on a chest of drawers were two large framed photographs: one of a woman whom Gautier recognized as Madame Hassler's mother and the other of a stout, elderly man, presumably her father.

'Now this is the room in which you told the intruders they could find money and jewelry?' Courtrand asked.

'Yes.'

'And what would they have found?'

'Not very much. A few thousand francs which I had drawn from the bank to pay the tradesmen on Monday and a little jewelry.' Josephine Hassler looked in the bureau and then pulled open the drawers of the chest. 'The money has gone. And look! Here are the empty jewel cases.'

She took the empty jewellers' boxes from the drawer and showed them to the two men. One was long and slim and had clearly held a necklace while the others were much smaller.

'Can you describe the missing pieces?' Gautier asked, his notebook ready.

'A diamond-and-sapphire necklace, a diamond pendant on a gold

27

chain and a gold brooch set with emeralds in the shape of a love-knot.'

'And nothing else was taken.'

Josephine Hassler hesitated for an instant, looked first at Courtrand and then at Gautier, and finally said: 'It was not jewels or money that they were really looking for.'

'Then what?'

'Papers. Come downstairs and I'll show you.'

The two men followed her downstairs into the dining-room. Like the drawing-room and Madame Hassler's bedroom it was furnished mainly with Louis XV and Louis XVI pieces and a fine Gobelin tapestry. Josephine Hassler pointed towards a heavy sideboard that stood against one wall.

'Would you two gentlemen be so kind as to move that please?'

Courtrand and Gautier moved the sideboard and found in the wall behind it a recess about one metre square and rather less than one metre in depth. It had been used as a substitute for a safe and was full of silver plate, two or three pieces of good china, some legal documents tied up with red ribbon and a brown-paper parcel.

Josephine Hassler pointed at the parcel. 'That was what the thieves were seeking. It contains papers that would fetch a large sum of money; all the letters which I received from the late president and copies of many of his private and confidential papers. He and I were working together on his memoirs, you know.' She paused and then added dramatically: 'I have reason to believe that certain foreign powers would pay a lot to lay their hands on those papers.'

'Yet even so the thieves left without them,' Gautier remarked.

'Yes. And do you know why? I made up a dummy parcel, just like that one, but filled only with old newspapers, business letters and bills. The parcel was in my bureau upstairs and that the thieves did take.'

'How would anyone have known that you had these private papers here? You might easily have had them kept in a bank.'

'That I cannot say.'

Courtrand said: 'If the thieves have failed in their objective, you must not ignore the possibility that they might return. You would be well advised, Madame, not to stay in this house alone.'

'My husband's cousin, Monsieur Charon, moved in with his wife last night. They will stay to chaperone me as long as I need them.' She smiled sadly. 'But to tell the truth, Monsieur Courtrand, the robbers have already taken all that I prize in life.'

'We have imposed on you too long, Madame,' Courtrand said.

'May I put one last question to you, Madame?' Gautier asked. 'I understand that on the night of the murders before retiring you, your husband and your mother all drank a glass of grog.'

'That's right.'

'What happened to the glasses, the bottle and the jug? They are not in any of these bedrooms.'

'I suppose Remy took them down to the kitchen.'

'He says he did not.'

Josephine looked at him defiantly. 'Then Remy must be wrong. He's very scatterbrained and forgetful, as you may have noticed. I can tell you one thing. I certainly didn't take them down.'

'Come now, Gautier, no more questions,' Courtrand said. 'Madame, we will leave you to go and rest. Take care of your health, please.'

IV

EARLY THE FOLLOWING afternoon Surat placed his report on
Gautier's desk. Anticipating his chief's surprise at the speed with
which he had completed the assignment, he remarked: 'It wasn't
difficult. Madame Hassler must be a talkative lady, with indiscreet
servants and curious neighbours.' Gautier told him to wait until he
had read the report.

Confidential Report
For the attention of Insp. Gautier
Madame Josephine Hassler (née Pinock) was born in or around
1860 (her claims as to her age vary considerably and this date is
no more than an estimate) in the village of Beaucourt which is
to be found not far from Montbéliard and close to the Swiss and
German borders. Her father was an industrialist who had been a
partner in the family firm of Pinock Frères, but his interest was
bought out by his brothers while he was still a young man.
Thereafter he led a life of leisure. Her mother Eva (née Stalan)
was the daughter of a local tavern keeper and her father was
considered to have married beneath himself. Indeed his marriage
and his intemperate drinking habits may have been the reason
why his brothers wanted to get him out of the family business.
At the age of eighteen Josephine was engaged for a very short
time to a young army officer, Lieutenant Mathurin. Her father
decided, however, that the lieutenant was too poor and the engagement was ended, which local people say provoked a storm of rage
on the part of the daughter.

Besides being beautiful, Josephine was very self-willed and it
is believed that she decided to revenge herself on her parents
and to escape from Beaucourt by marrying Félix Hassler. Hassler

was twenty years older than her and by profession a painter of stained-glass windows, whom she met while he was working in Bayonne Cathedral. He was neither good-looking nor wealthy and his main attraction to Josephine was that he owned a house in Paris.

After their marriage, they came to live in the house in Impasse Louvain and Josephine, having quickly got rid of her husband's sister who was living with him, set about turning her husband from an artisan into an artist. He became a portrait painter and before very long a number of prosperous businessmen were commissioning his services. Since his talent was more than limited, the general view is that the businessmen were more interested in Madame Hassler than in her husband's painting and that the commissions were an ingenious way of paying for the favours which they received from her.

Madame Hassler's ambitions did not stop there and she then began building for herself a reputation as a hostess. Although her salon was attended in the main by only mediocre literary and artistic figures and the wealthy bourgeoisie, she appears from time to time to have attracted to her house more eminent men, some of them in important positions. Those whose names have been mentioned in this connection include: The former Attorney General, the President of the Senate, the British Ambassador, Marshal Gallifet and Judge Bertin.

The general impression among neighbours and tradesmen is that the Hasslers live well above their income and in a more or less permanent state of debt. The shortage of money and Madame Hassler's extravagances are thought to be the cause of many bitter arguments between the couple. They have one daughter, Marguerite, aged seventeen, who recently became engaged to a son of the Delaisse family who are in business making automobiles.

'Excellent!' Gautier told Surat when he had finished reading the report. 'This is exactly what I wanted.'

'And will it help?'

'It gives us a starting point. Someone went to the Hasslers' house that evening and whoever it was didn't break in. From what the manservant Mansard says, I believe it may have been one of Josephine's gentlemen friends.'

'But would he have gone there knowing that her husband and her mother were in the house?'

'Very possibly. I rather think that Hassler turned a blind eye to his wife's infidelities. Anyway, keep working on these lines. Make enquiries among the neighbours and servants of all the men listed in your report. Someone may know something, a coachman perhaps who drove to Impasse Louvain that evening. And see that the local police ask around among the fiacre drivers. But be discreet. Some of the men are important people and we don't want them to start complaining to the Minister of Justice.'

'I take it that you don't believe Madame Hassler's story?'

'Men in long beards carrying lanterns? The woman must be simple if she hopes anyone believes that tale!'

He scarcely finished speaking when Courtrand came into the office, followed by Nordel. The director looked uncommonly pleased and Nordel wore the quiet, complacent smile of a schoolboy who has at last managed to ingratiate himself with a difficult headmaster.

'Have you heard, Gautier?' asked Courtrand. 'The robes which the thieves who broke into Madame Hassler's house were wearing have been traced.'

'Are you sure?'

'Tell him, Nordel.'

Although he obviously had no need to, Nordel consulted his notebook as he explained that a firm of theatrical costumiers had six weeks ago rented a consignment of costumes, including six robes to be worn by Jewish Levites, to the Hebrew Theatre in Paris for its production of the play *Cain and Abel*. The play's run had ended the previous week and when the costumiers had collected the batch of costumes three of the robes had been missing. The wardrobe mistress of the theatre had told the police that only three of the Levites' robes had actually been used in the production, the remaining three being held in reserve. She also admitted that about ten days previously she had lent these three robes to a friend who had wished to wear them to a fancy-dress ball.

'That could just be coincidence,' Gautier suggested.

'Ah, there's more to come,' Courtrand replied. 'The man who borrowed the robes is an American painter named York and we have established that his mistress is an artist's model who in the past has posed for Félix Hassler.'

Courtrand paused. Then with the air of an actor who had a final dramatic line which he will not deliver until the audience is hushed and expectant, he added slowly: 'The American, York, has a red beard.'

V

GAUTIER SAT NEXT to Josephine Hassler in a closed carriage stationed in Rue Blanche. From where they were waiting, he could see the icing-sugar dome of the great church of Sacré Coeur, built after the last war by the French in a mood of piety and as an act of expiation for the sins which, many people believed, had brought about the country's defeat by the arrogant, new nation of Germany. He could also see opposite them in Place Blanche, the impresario Ziddler's enterprise, the Moulin Rouge, with its great replica of a red windmill above the entrance. It was neither the church nor the dance hall, however, which held his attention but Chez Adèle, a small, unpretentious café on the corner of a narrow street that ran into Place Blanche. It was at Chez Adèle that the American artist York was supposed to lunch every day, very often accompanied by the model Claudine.

'How will we know when they go into the café?' Josephine Hassler asked. 'We are too far away here to see.'

'Two of my men in plain clothes are already in the café. When the man York goes in, one of them will come out and signal to me. You and I will then go into Chez Adèle by the back entrance and it has been arranged that you will be able to look at this man from the kitchen without his seeing you.'

In the 24 hours which had elapsed since the loss of the Levites' robes had been reported, the police had been able to track down the painter, York, without much difficulty. He was living in a studio in Rue Cortot and was well known in Montmartre if for no other reason because, unlike most of the other artists living around him, he received a regular income from his family in the United States and was a soft touch for a drink or a meal or a loan to buy paints. He was also reputed to be a man of monotonously regular

34

habits, frequenting the same bistros every day and lunching always at Chez Adèle.

Madame Hassler had been told by Courtrand to make herself look inconspicuous in a district where a well-dressed woman would soon attract stares and she had put on a long black cloak over her clothes and wore a black toque. As they had driven through Paris towards Montmartre, Gautier found that he was aware of her physical presence next to him. Once or twice as the carriage rattled over the cobblestones or swung round a corner, he felt the pressure of her thigh or her knee against his own. He sensed then why men should find her seductive, particularly middle-aged men, for she combined with an almost animal attraction, an air of simplicity and directness which could easily have been mistaken for innocence.

After they had been waiting half-an-hour or so, he saw a couple entering Chez Adèle and a few minutes later a man in a brown suit and a brown bowler hat, whom he recognized as Nordel came out, walked a few yards along the pavement and held up a folded newspaper. That was the signal for Josephine Hassler and himself to move. Leaving the carriage, they crossed to the other side of the Rue Blanche where they would be less visible to people sitting in Chez Adèle and made their way towards the back door of the café.

The kitchen was small, primitive and far from clean but the smells rising from the pans and casseroles on the stove were not unappetizing. A small, wizened man in a dirty apron, the husband of the formidable Adèle, was skinning a rabbit and when he saw Gautier he pointed with his knife towards a curtain of orange beads which separated the kitchen from the main part of the café.

'You can see from there, Monsieur.'

Gautier led Madame Hassler across the kitchen to a point where they could see through the bead curtain. The interior of the café was small and gloomy, with less than a dozen tables, but it was crowded. About half of the clientèle were working people, artisans, carters and girls who spent their evenings in the Moulin Rouge or the Elysée Montmartre trying to contrive chance encounters with men, while the other half were either artists or people with artistic pretensions.

Gautier recognized York from a photograph which he had been shown at Sûreté headquarters earlier that morning. The American was slight, with a thin, consumptive face. His hair, which he wore long and his straggly beard were of a sandy colour which, at a stretch of the imagination might have been described as red. He was wearing a dark-green corduroy suit and a pair of handsome cowboy boots. At a time when most of the artists in Montmartre wore clogs or tennis shoes and when Picasso's mistress Fernande Olivier was forced to stay in his studio for several weeks since she could not afford to buy a pair of shoes, it was the boots more than anything which marked York out for what he was, a rich American amateur.

The girl with him, whom Gautier took to be the model, Claudine Verdurin, wore a long strawberry-coloured dress, gathered loosely at the waist, and sandals. Her dark-brown hair was tied in an untidy knot above the back of her neck with a black-velvet ribbon and her face, although not beautiful, had a certain insolent charm. Looking at her, Gautier could almost imagine that one of the urchin children of Montmartre whom Poulbot painted so expressively had suddenly blossomed into maturity.

'That's the man,' Gautier told Josephine Hassler. 'The one sitting at the table in the far corner with a girl. Look at him carefully and tell me if you recognize him.'

'He certainly looks very like one of the men who broke into my bedroom.'

'Take your time, Madame. If you are not absolutely certain, say so.'

Josephine hesitated and then said: 'Yes, it is the same man. I'm sure of it. And that girl. She's the one who was with the men and wanted to kill me.'

'But you said that woman was ugly and had black, frizzy hair.'

'She must have been wearing a wig. That's the same woman, I'll swear on it.'

'Right. The two of them must not see you, so will you please be kind enough to stay here, Madame, and in a few minutes one of my men will drive you to your home.'

Gautier passed through the bead curtain into the restaurant. Although the café's only toilet was at the back and anyone wishing to use it would have to return through the kitchen, three or four of the clients looked sharply at him as he came into the room. A certain class of Parisian, he sometimes believed, had the gift of being able to smell a policeman. As he drew near to the American, the sound of conversation fell noticeably.

'Are you Monsieur Edward York?'

'Yes. That's me.'

'Inspector Gautier of the Sûreté. We wish to ask you a few questions. Would you be so kind as to come with me.'

'Can't you ask them here?'

Gautier nodded in the direction of the other people in the café. 'I think you would prefer it if we discussed the matter elsewhere.'

The American began to look truculent. 'Say, what is this? Am I being arrested?'

'I hope that will not be necessary, Monsieur.'

'I insist that the United States Consul be informed. You have no right to treat an American citizen in this way!'

'At this stage we only wish to ask you some questions. Should it be decided to detain you, then of course your Consul will be told.'

'You had better go with him, Eddie,' the girl said resignedly. 'Nobody ever wins arguing with the flics.'

'Are you Claudine Verdurin?' Gautier asked her.

'That's right.'

'Then I'd like you to come as well, Mademoiselle.'

'Now look here!' York began to protest but the girl laid a hand on his arm.

'That's all right. I have no objection to coming with you. But must we come immediately? We're only halfway through a good meal.'

Gautier pulled a chair up to the table and sat down with them. 'I don't mind waiting, Mademoiselle.'

What he was doing was right outside the rules, he knew that, and he knew that Courtrand would be outraged if he were to hear of it, for Courtrand believed that all his men should always and unquestioningly follow the rule book. Gautier also knew that on occasions one gained more by being flexible and there were times when he deliberately bent the rules just to prove to himself that Courtrand was wrong.

'A reasonable policeman!' Claudine exclaimed. 'We must look after this rare specimen, Eddie. Give him some wine.'

37

The thin edge of sarcasm in her tone suggested that she was challenging Gautier but he did not take offence. Instead he accepted the glass of vin ordinaire which York poured out for him and as he sipped it, watched the two people he was supposed to be arresting finish their meal. The American was clearly ill-at-ease, frightened no doubt by this unexpected confrontation with the police, but Claudine appeared relaxed and chatted freely as she ate. In manner, if not in appearance, she was very unlike most of the artists' models who were to be met in and around Place Blanche, where there existed an unofficial market for models and where a painter could find a model for almost any subject from the Infant Moses to Our Lady of Mercy. The female models whom Gautier knew were for the most part good-natured, unintelligent girls who had chosen the profession through vanity and laziness or in some cases for the opportunities that it provided for casual sex. Claudine Verdurin, on the other hand, seemed free of affectation, direct and determined.

'What's all this about, anyway?' York asked Gautier, encouraged by the policeman's informal manner.

'The Juge d'Instruction will tell you that.'

'Juge d'Instruction!' Claudine exclaimed. 'Then it's a criminal matter?'

'Can't you give us an indication of what he is going to ask us?'

Gautier decided that as he had already cut across protocol once, a little further trespassing could do no harm. He told them: 'All I will say is this. We're interested in the robes which you, Monsieur, borrowed from the Hebrew Theatre and why you haven't returned them.'

Claudine looked at him incredulously and then began to laugh.

VI

MINISTRY OF JUSTICE

Account of interrogation by the Juge d'Instruction

Crime at No. 8, Impasse Louvain   Dossier No. 0008

On Wednesday, 4 June, before us, Bertin, appeared Edward York and Claudine Verdurin, both of Montmartre in the City of Paris and were examined as follows:

Question: It has been established and is the subject of sworn statements by others that you, York, took possession six weeks ago of three Jewish ecclesiastical robes, the property of Roland Fils, costumiers, when they were on hire to the Hebrew Theatre in Paris. Do you York deny this assertion?

York: No. I admit that I did borrow the robes.

Question: And for what purpose may I ask?

York: Some friends of mine and I were going to a masquerade ball. We had the idea that we might dress ourselves to represent some biblical theme. One suggestion that we might go as Abraham and Isaac. Another idea was Christ scourging the money-lenders.

Question: Did you use the costumes for this purpose?

York: In the end we only used one of them. My other friends decided not to go to the ball at all so Mademoiselle Verdurin and I went dressed as Joseph and Mary.

Question: And you Mademoiselle Verdurin, do you confirm that this was the purpose for which you borrowed the costumes and that you accompanied Monsieur York to this ball?

Verdurin: The answer is 'Yes' to both questions.

39

Question: If, as you say, you borrowed the robes, why did you not return them? And where are they now?

York: I guess I just never got round to it. As far as I know the robes are still lying around somewhere in my studio.

Question: That can be established in due course. For the present I have a question for Mademoiselle Verdurin. Is it true that you knew the painter Félix Hassler?

Verdurin: I don't believe so.

Question: His widow claims – and this is substantiated by his account books – that you acted as model for Hassler just eighteen months ago. Are you denying this?

Verdurin: Not at all. It is quite possible. I work for a good many artists and I certainly do not remember them all. Where is his studio?

Question: At Number 8 Impasse Louvain, just off rue de Vaugirard. Do you still deny sitting for him?

Verdurin: No, I do remember the house and also the man. A little fellow with a very German head who looked more like a bourgeois shopkeeper than a painter. I think I did a couple of days for him when one of his regular models was sick.

Question: And did you not remember all this when you heard of his death?

Verdurin: Is he dead?

Question: Come, Mademoiselle, surely you're not pretending that you have not heard of Félix Hassler's murder? All the newspapers are full of the Impasse Louvain affair.

Verdurin: Why should I read the newspapers? They are of no interest to me. We're not great readers of newspapers up on the Butte.

Question: And you, Monsieur York, have you not heard of the murder?

York: Wasn't that the double murder? An artist and an old lady, his mother-in-law?

Question: Madame Hassler, widow of the dead man, has identified you Monsieur and you Mademoiselle, as two of the people who broke into her house to steal money and documents and who, in the course of the robbery, killed her husband and mother, threatened her life and left her gagged and bound. Do you admit this?

York: Us? Robbery and murder? Is this woman crazy?

Verdurin: Certainly we deny these accusations. Categorically and in every detail.

Question: We shall see as to that. It is the belief of the police that when you modelled for the dead man, you discovered that he had money and his wife jewels and valuable papers. Having learnt the geography of the house, you thought it would be easy to rob it, having first disguised yourselves; you, York, and another man in the Jewish robes, and you, Verdurin, with a wig and paint. It may be that you had already stolen a key to the house or you may have had an accomplice among the servants. What is your answer to that?

York: It's crazy! Absolutely crazy!

Verdurin: And are we permitted to know when this robbery and these murders took place?

Question: On the night of Saturday last, the thirty-first of May at midnight. Can you account for your movements on that day?

Verdurin: I can. I was in London.

Question: For what purpose?

Verdurin: Not long ago I posed for an English artist, Sir Frank Knowles, while he was in Paris. He was not able to finish the painting here and paid my expenses to go over to London so he could complete it. I crossed over on the channel steamer last Wednesday and returned only on Monday morning.

Question: And is there anyone who can confirm this?

Verdurin: Sir Frank himself or the hotel in which I stayed, the Museum Court Hotel in Bloomsbury.

York: I was not in Paris either! I spent the weekend in the Midi at St Tropez. A friend of mine, the Spanish artist, Pablo Munoz, has rented a cottage there for the summer. I stayed with him from Friday to Monday.

Question: This too will have to be confirmed. If you will give us your friend's address we will telegraph the local police and send them round to make enquiries.

The two who had been questioned then wrote down the names and addresses of the people whom they claimed could corroborate their stories.

Read and signed by:
Verdurin
York
Bertin

VII

NOT LONG AFTER the interrogation of York and Claudine
Verdurin had been concluded, Gautier strolled from his office
down to the Café Corneille in Boulevard St Germain. Like most
of the better known cafés in Paris, the Corneille had its own particular clientèle, a group of habitués who used the place as a kind
of unofficial club. In the case of the Corneille, the habitués were
mainly writers and lawyers, with a sprinkling of more discerning
and more acceptable journalists.

Although he had never really understood why, Gautier had
found himself also accepted in the group. Some of his colleagues
in the Sûreté had hinted that a policeman who mixed with the
intelligentsia must have ideas above his station. He ignored the
hints because he had discovered quite by chance that the Prefect of
Police, who was, after all, head of the whole police organization,
approved. Some months previously he had met the prefect, Lépic,
in the Café Corneille.

'It's Inspector Gautier, isn't it?' Lépic had recognized him and
later when they were alone for a moment he had added: 'I'm pleased
to notice that you are evidently at home and well liked in this
excellent café, Inspector. We in the police must learn to be inte-
grated in society and not a force apart.'

Gautier suspected that Lépic, whom everyone recognized as an
unusually shrewd and able man, was also well aware that cafés
rather than fashionable drawing-rooms were the real centres of
political thought in France and, in some cases, of subversive ideas.
It was not for nothing that the government, in times of unrest or
discontent, sent spies and agents to mingle with people in the
cafés of Paris.

This evening he had timed his arrival at the Café Corneille

well, for the man he had been hoping to see could not himself have been there very long since he was still alone at a table. Pierre Duthrey was a journalist on the staff of *Figaro* and a man whose knowledge and judgement Gautier had come to respect. They had done each other small favours more than once in the past and had built up a mutual trust almost strong enough to be called an understanding.

Gautier joined Duthrey at his table, ordered a café and a brandy and they exchanged the courtesies which come so readily to Frenchmen, each enquiring after the other's state of health and then after the other's wife and family.

Then Gautier asked: 'What is the press thinking about the affair at Impasse Louvain?'

'Most of us are just sitting waiting for something to happen.'

'And what do you imagine might happen?'

Duthrey frowned, as though he were trying to crystallize his own ideas. 'The newspapers are divided about that. Some, like *Figaro*, believe that Madame Hassler's story is so preposterous that no sane person can be expected to believe it and that quite soon the real truth will explode. But there's another school of thought which maintains that no one could possibly have invented such a bizarre and improbable tale and that therefore it must be true. They believe that soon the police will track down and arrest the criminals.'

'What is your personal view?'

'That politics are mixed up in this. Madame Hassler has powerful friends. You will know of course that the Juge d'Instruction in the case, Bertin, used to frequent her salon and they also say that your chief, Courtrand, is unusually well disposed towards her. *Le Matin*, a paper which always supported the late president, is sparing no effort to present Madame Hassler in the most favourable light. Given all these circumstances, I fear we may never be allowed to know the truth.'

Gautier made no comment. Through loyalty to his superiors he did not wish to say anything that might suggest that Duthrey's analysis of the situation was very like his own. He was saved from having to discuss the matter any further, for the time being at least, by the timely arrival of other friends who came to join

44

them at their table. The murders at Impasse Louvain had not yet caught the attention of the public as one might have expected, mainly because all Paris was still talking of another sensation. The Duc de Limoges, head of one of France's leading families and more nobly born than much of Europe's royalty, had only a few days previously obtained a legal separation from his American wife on the grounds of her lesbian relationship with a well-known actress.

One of the regulars at the Café Corneille who had just joined Gautier and Duthrey, was a young lawyer and for the next twenty minutes he kept them entertained with scabrous and highly improbable stories of the legal proceedings. The evening was passing pleasantly enough until the arrival of another journalist, Charles Cros of *Le Matin*. Small, cocky and abrasive, Cros was a man whom Gautier both disliked and distrusted. Unlike Duthrey, the man from *Le Matin* was always ready to take advantage of a friendship or to betray a confidence if it would lead him to a headline.

'So my paper was right?' He asked Gautier with belligerent cheerfulness as soon as he had sat down at the table.

'In what respect?'

'All along we have maintained that Josephine Hassler did not murder her husband, in spite of the accusations that some newspapers were only too ready to level at her.'

'Are you saying that her innocence has been established?' Duthrey asked him.

'Hasn't your pal the inspector told you? She has identified two of the people who robbed and attacked her and the disguises which they used that night have been found.'

'Is this true?' Duthrey asked Gautier.

'I cannot comment on a matter which is under judicial examination.'

Cros laughed delightedly, emptied his glass of absinthe and banged it on the table to catch the attention of the waiter. 'Better and better! If the police are still keeping this under wraps then *Le Matin* will have an exclusive story. Come, my friends, won't all of you take a glass of wine with me to celebrate? You'll read the full story tomorrow.'

Half-an-hour later Gautier and Duthrey were alone again, this time walking away from the Café Corneille where Cros was still noisily inviting all around him to join in celebrating his scoop. They went towards the corner of the boulevard where a line of fiacres stood waiting, for Duthrey intended to return to the offices of *Figaro*.

'Soon all the fiacres will be driven off the streets by these accursed motor cars,' Duthrey was saying. 'There was a nasty accident in the Champs Elysées this morning when a horse pulling a fiacre took fright at a passing motor car and bolted. A woman passenger in the fiacre was thrown out right under the wheels of a passing calèche.'

'The motor omnibus will be the one to kill off the fiacres. Some idiot is already designing one.'

'Has anyone stopped to think what that would mean for horses and horse breeders? Why, the Omnibus Company of Paris alone has nearly 20,000 horses in service.'

'*Figaro* should start a campaign against the motor omnibus.'

'That's scarcely likely. Our director is crazy about combustion engines. He has already bought one of the new Dion automobiles.'

'Then why don't we sell the idea to Cros?' Gautier used this device to turn the conversation round to Cros, because he knew Duthrey would be too tactful to do so. 'After defending Madame Hassler, *Le Matin* can fight a battle for the horse.'

Duthrey allowed a few moments to pass before he accepted the opening. 'I wonder where he got that story which he was just crowing about.'

'Not from us or the Ministry of Justice, so it could only have come from Madame Hassler herself.'

'Then it's true?'

'I'm not a journalist,' Gautier said, choosing his words deliberately, 'but if I were, my report in tomorrow's paper would read something like this: "Certain newspapers in Paris are today carrying a story to the effect that two of the criminals who broke into the house of Félix Hassler in Impasse Louvain last Saturday night and left him dead, as well as his mother-in-law, have been positively identified by his widow. We understand from a most

46

reliable source that this is not the case. Two people were in fact questioned by the authorities yesterday evening, but they were able to satisfy the examining magistrate that they had played no part in the crime and they were not detained." '

Duthrey pulled a notebook from his pocket and jotted down the essentials of what Gautier had told him. He laughed as he stepped into the first fiacre in the line. 'Let me know when I can do you a favour, Jean-Paul.'

Dressed entirely in black and with her face hidden behind a heavy black veil, Josephine Hassler came into Gautier's office looking like an actor playing Death in a medieval allegorical play. When she lifted the veil, however, it was to reveal not the pallor of death but a face flushed with indignation and eyes alight with anger.

'I insist on seeing the director,' she told Gautier imperiously.

'Monsieur Courtrand will not be here for half-an-hour or more, Madame,' Gautier replied.

'It's monstrous! Insufferable! Will you police never take any action? How long do we have to wait before you find the assassins of my husband and my dear mother?'

'We are doing everything we can, Madame.'

'You think so?' Her words were hard and bright, with the cutting edge of diamonds. 'Then let me tell you this, Inspector. I have friends who will see to it that you do much more, that you begin to pursue this case with energy and zeal instead of sitting indolently in your offices. People high above you, Monsieur; attorneys, judges, ministers even, will hear of how you are failing in your duty. Why should I have to endure the sneers and suspicions of the world while the real criminals remain at large and you idle your time away?'

As she stormed on, Gautier watched her. She was right when she said that little progress had been made in the case by the Sûreté. It was equally true that the press had been growing increasingly cynical about the affair at Impasse Louvain and more than one newspaper had declared openly that Josephine Hassler's story was not to be believed and that she herself must be implicated in the crime. Even so, Gautier found himself wondering whether her show of indignation was genuine or whether her visit to the Sûreté that morning was another carefully-staged performance, designed to convince the police of her innocence.

During the last day or so he had thought a good deal about the case and about what tactics the police should follow. So far they had been following routine procedure, checking possible leads and any facts which might corroborate Josephine Hassler's account of what had happened at her house that evening. Now in his own mind, he was planning a new strategy, one based on the assumption that her whole story had been a string of lies. He had started to re-read everything in the dossier of the case, his notes, her statements, the reports of his subordinates and of the laboratories to see what evidence he could find which would incriminate her.

'Our task has been made more difficult by you yourself, Madame,' he said coldly.

'What on earth can you possibly mean?'

'The accusations which you made against the American York and the girl Verdurin wasted a great deal of the department's time.'

'I only said I thought they were the people who had broken into our house.'

'We are as anxious as you are to discover who murdered your husband, Madame. And there is one way in which you can help us.'

'What is that?'

'The best chance of tracking down thieves in a case of robbery is by finding the missing property and that is not as difficult as you might imagine. There are only a limited number of ways in which a thief can dispose of stolen property and in cases where the robbery was accompanied by murder, it becomes even more difficult. Those who make a living out of handling stolen goods never like becoming involved in murder. It would help us if we had a detailed description of the jewelry which was stolen from you, so we knew exactly what to search for.'

Josephine Hassler's hesitation was only momentary. She looked at Gautier and he wondered whether she suspected that he might be trying to trap her into a lie. 'You already have a description of the pieces which were taken from my boudoir.'

'Yes, but what about the rest? Your rings and your mother's jewelry?'

She responded by describing each piece of jewelry and Gautier wrote down the descriptions. One of her three rings, she said, had been gold set with diamonds and sapphires, the second an eternity ring and the third a large solitaire emerald set in a claw mounting. Her mother's wedding ring had her name and the date of the marriage inscribed on the inside of the gold band while the brooch was an oval shape set with pearls.

'Counting the three pieces missing from your boudoir, that makes eight items altogether?'

'That's correct.'

'Right. We'll have the list copied and send policemen round with it to every jeweller in Paris whom we know to be engaged in dubious business.'

'I hope you are successful, Inspector.' Josephine Hassler's wrath appeared to have abated by this time and her tone was much friendlier as she went on: 'No one can possibly understand how my daughter and I are suffering and will continue to suffer until those who did this dreadful thing are caught.'

'So your daughter is back in Paris, then?'

'Yes, the poor darling. And it is mainly for her sake that I want this affair brought to a speedy conclusion. You know she is to be married?'

'No, I didn't know.'

'Yes, to a wonderful young man of very good family. And they have agreed not to see each other until this vile business is over and our family's name has been cleared.'

'That seems unduly harsh.'

'Not at all. It's a question of principle, one might say of honour. We can't allow the young man's family to be embarrassed by the scandal and by the newspaper publicity. So think of my poor darling Meg, Inspector, and of the price she is having to pay. Think of her unhappiness even if you cannot think of mine.'

She treated Gautier to a persuasive, almost imploring smile. It was as though she had been probing for his most vulnerable points and, deciding he was not a man to be bullied, was now trying out her weapons of feminine appeal. She was one of those women, Gautier decided, who had developed the art of giving a man the impression that she lived alone in a delicious, secret world which he, and only he, was being invited to share.

Soon, he felt, she would have been asking for promises, but before she reached the point of exploiting his chivalry, a policeman came into the room with a message. The director had arrived in his office and would be only too delighted to see Madame Hassler.

After she had left his room, Gautier sent for Surat and told him: 'I want that woman followed when she leaves the Sûreté, but not by any of us. Do you know of anyone who could do it discreetly?'

'I have just the man. He's always to be found at the café around the corner and I've used him before. He'll do anything for five francs.'

'I should hope so. That's twice what many people earn in a day. You'll need to give him money for fiacres as well, because Josephine Hassler is not the type to travel in anything so vulgar as an omnibus. Hurry along and fix it up. She may not be with the director more than half-an-hour or so.'

Surat left and Gautier made out a list of all the jewelry which Josephine Hassler had claimed had been stolen from her house with an exact description of each piece. He sent the list to be copied with instructions that a copy should be circulated to the police commissariat in every arrondissement, while at the same time three men should start making a tour of every disreputable jeweller in the city to see whether any of the pieces had already been sold.

He had scarcely completed these arrangements and was about to resume his study of the dossier of the case when another messenger arrived from Courtrand.

'The director wants this statement circulated to all daily newspapers,' he told Gautier, holding out a sheet of paper.

The statement read:

The Director of the Sûreté wishes it to be known that the rumours now circulating to the effect that Madame Josephine Hassler was implicated in the murder of her husband and her mother are entirely without foundation. The police have ample evidence to show that the murders were committed by intruders who broke into the Hasslers' house to rob them and they are confident that the criminals will be apprehended in the very near future.

Signed: Courtrand.

When the messenger had left and he was alone, Gautier put his hands over his eyes in despair and exclaimed: 'Mother of God! The man's gone off his head!'

VIII

NEXT MORNING SURAT came into Gautier's office with the report of the agent whom he had hired to follow Josephine Hassler. After leaving the Sûreté, she had apparently gone to a couturier in Rue St Honoré where she had spent almost two hours. From there she had walked to the Ritz Hotel, stopping at two or three shops on the way. Surat's man had not thought of making a note of the names of these shops – he was not after all trained in police work – but one of them had been a jewellers, he was sure of that. When she reached the Rue Cambon entrance of the Ritz, he had wisely made no attempt to follow her into the hotel, realizing that he would never have got past the doorman. Instead he had made a few enquiries in a nearby café to which the chambermaids and waiters from the Ritz often slipped out for a drink. From there he had learned that the lady in the black veil had been shown up to a private apartment where she had lunched with a certain Colonel de Clermont. She had spent almost three hours in the Ritz and on leaving had been driven in a fiacre straight home.

'Interesting!' Gautier commented when Surat had delivered the report. 'And have you been able to find out anything about this colonel?'

'Only that he stays fairly frequently at the Ritz and has a home in the country, the Château d'Ivry.'

'Nothing more?'

'The Château d'Ivry is situated not far from Beaucourt, the village where Madame Hassler was born.'

'Even more interesting! This colonel must be a very special friend of the Hassler woman if only a few days after her husband is murdered she is indiscreet enough to go and lunch with him and unchaperoned at that. We must get to know more about him.'

'How, patron?'

'Go down to the Château d'Ivry and make enquiries, but tactfully. At this stage it will be better if our colonel doesn't know that we're interested in him. And while you're there go to Beaucourt as well. The local gossips may know of a connection between the Hassler woman and the colonel. Perhaps they were lovers when she was young. Find out whatever you can.'

'Well, I hope I have more luck there than we've had in Paris so far.'

The tone of this last remark, a compound of pessimism and cynicism, was quite out of character for Surat, and Gautier recognized in his subordinate's mood a reflection of his own. Everyone in the Sûreté who had been working on the Impasse Louvain case was beginning to be infected by the same feeling. No one liked the case. No progress was being made, every attempt to trace the criminals had ended abortively, the search for the stolen jewelry had proved fruitless. Policemen were beginning to suspect that they were working on a dead case, one which they were not expected nor even required to solve. So they went through the motions of working on it, but without enthusiasm and without conviction. What made matters worse was that the press were now openly saying that there was a conspiracy to conceal the truth and that people in high places were being protected.

For some days now Gautier had thought it was his duty to speak to the Director on the subject. Cynicism led to a loss of morale which, although it might not affect the outcome of the Impasse Louvain case, would be damaging to future efficiency. Courtrand appeared totally unaware of the sense of malaise in the department and remained urbane, pompous and confident; so confident that Gautier found himself wondering whether his own judgement might be at fault and had said nothing.

Now he decided that he could procrastinate no longer and must speak frankly to his chief. Leaving his room he went down to the director's office on the first floor and there he found Courtrand speaking on the telephone. Although the telephone was rapidly becoming more common in Paris and all police stations and offices were now equipped with it, the system seldom worked smoothly. A caller was at the mercy of the telephone operators who were an autocratic breed, only giving their favours in rare moments of good humour and disconnecting a call or even refusing to put one through, if a subscriber should make so much as a hint of a complaint.

Today Courtrand was having difficulty with his call and more than once felt obliged to remind the operator of his authority and importance. After several interruptions he eventually concluded his conversation and put down the instrument.

'That was a journalist speaking to me from Madame Hassler's house,' he told Gautier. 'There has been a most important development in the case.'

'What's that?'

'The manservant has been caught with some of the stolen property in his possession.'

'I hope this is not going to be another false accusation.'

'You're too sceptical by far, Gautier.' Courtrand crossed the room to fetch his hat and gloves which he always kept on a small table by the door, and his frock coat which hung near them. 'The stolen jewelry was found in Mansard's wallet,' he told Gautier, 'And there were two journalists present when it happened.'

'How very convenient!' An instinct fashioned over long years of dealing with crimes and criminals told him to distrust this unlikely coincidence. He remembered that only the previous day he and Josephine Hassler had discussed the matter of the stolen jewelry.

'We must both get down to Impasse Louvain at once,' Courtrand told him.

They drove to the Hasslers' house in a fiacre. Public interest in the Impasse Louvain affair had swollen enormously since *Le Matin*'s sensational story of the arrest of York and Claudine Verdurin and its subsequent rebuttal. All the daily newspapers were giving the case headline coverage and a fair-sized crowd were gathered outside the house when they arrived. Someone in the mob recognized Courtrand and a voice from the back of the throng shouted jeering abuse.

'Hey, Monsieur le Director, is this a professional visit or have you come to renew your intimate friendship with the lady?'

'Intimate friendship? More likely carnal knowledge.'

54

'He'll have to take his turn then,' another voice jeered. 'She takes her lovers in order of precedence, the president first.'

'Why don't you arrest the whore?' A woman screamed. 'She's the one who killed her husband. And her own mother, cruel bitch!'

Three policemen were standing guard outside the gate of the house and with their help Courtrand and Gautier managed to elbow a path through the crowd. Gautier noticed that all the policemen were big, husky men which was a sure sign that the superintendent of the arrondissement was expecting trouble.

Inside the drawing-room of the house several people were assembled, waiting for them. Besides Josephine Hassler, Gautier recognized Cros and another journalist from *Le Matin,* a pretty, nervous girl of about seventeen whom he assumed to be the Hasslers' daughter, a middle-aged couple and the manservant Mansard. The couple were introduced as the cousins of Félix Hassler, a Monsieur Charon and his wife, who were now living in the house since, as Josephine Hassler explained, she and her daughter were afraid to live alone with a hostile crowd outside. The manservant stood apart from the rest of the party, looking pale and frightened.

'Now, what's all this about?' Courtrand demanded.

'Monsieur le Directeur,' Cros began formally, as though he were already addressing a jury. 'This fellow Mansard was asked in our presence to produce and open his wallet. Inside we found this.' He handed Courtrand an object wrapped in tissue paper. 'The discovery was witnessed by myself and my colleague as well as by Monsieur and Madame Charon. Naturally we will be ready to make sworn statements to that effect.'

After unwrapping the tissue paper, Courtrand held in the palm of his hand an oval brooch of pearls set in gold. He looked towards Josephine Hassler. 'And is this yours, Madame?'

'Not mine, no. It belonged to my mother. The inspector will remember that it was one of the pieces of jewelry I described to him only yesterday for the list of stolen property he was compiling.'

Courtrand turned towards Mansard. 'Do you admit stealing this brooch?'

'No! No!' Mansard shook his head in agitation. 'I've never even seen it before.'

55

'Then how did it come to be in your wallet?'

'Someone must have put it there, Monsieur.'

'You scoundrel!' Courtrand exclaimed. 'Are you insolent enough to suggest that it was one of these people here?' He waved a hand in the general direction of Madame Hassler and her relatives. 'Are you saying that they would have deliberately tried to implicate you in this affair?'

'I don't know who put it there, but I tell you I never stole it.'

'A likely story!' Cros scoffed. 'When would anyone have had an opportunity to plant the brooch in your wallet? Why don't you confess that you were the accomplice of those criminals who murdered your master? Give us their names and then perhaps the director will see that things go easier for you. Instead of being guillotined for conspiracy to murder, you may merely end up in prison.'

Mansard began to tremble with fear and his face twitched so violently that he could scarcely speak. 'It isn't true! I know nothing about this!' He looked at Gautier imploringly. 'Tell them that I'm innocent Monsieur l'Inspecteur. You know I've done no wrong.'

'What impertinence!' Cros laughed derisively. 'Now he's appealing for police protection!'

Gautier could see that Cros was thoroughly enjoying the central part which he had been called upon to play in the scene, a scene which in all probability he had contrived. The man was an egotist and when the story came to be written in *Le Matin*, he would give himself all the credit for finding the stolen jewels and putting the police on the right track to find the murderers of the Impasse Louvain affair. From the moment they had arrived, Courtrand should have taken a firm stand against this attempt to interfere in a police investigation. As it was Cros was now in charge, asking the questions and ready to pronounce a verdict.

'In what circumstances was the jewelry found?' Gautier asked Josephine Hassler.

'What do you mean?'

'Who searched this man's wallet and why?'

'What does that matter?' Cros demanded. 'You have the evidence so what more do you need?'

56

Ignoring him, Gautier addressed himself squarely to Josephine Hassler. 'Was it you, Madame?'

'Allow me to ask the questions, Inspector,' Courtrand said and his tone made it clear that this was a reprimand. 'Madame, would you be so kind as to tell me who actually found the brooch in this man's possession?'

'I did.'

'In the presence of these gentlemen?' Courtrand pointed towards the journalists.

'Yes. And my husband's cousin and his wife were here too.'

'But why did you decide to look in Mansard's wallet? And was it not rather convenient that these gentlemen from the newspaper were here at the time?'

Josephine Hassler flushed and for a moment Gautier thought she was going to lose her temper. Then, controlling her emotions, she said slowly: 'It didn't happen like that.'

'Then tell me what did happen, Madame.'

'Yesterday I was discussing the murders with Monsieur Cros and he pointed out, as many of my friends have, that the people who killed my dear husband must almost certainly have had an accomplice who let them into the house. And the more I thought about this, the more likely it seemed that the accomplice must be Remy. For one thing he has never been able to explain why he did not come down to help us when we were being attacked that night. It's quite inconceivable that he did not hear the noise that those dreadful people were making. I remembered also that several times he told us contradictory stories about himself: the town where he was born, his childhood and the jobs he has previously held. This morning I mentioned my suspicions to Monsieur Charon here and it was he who suggested that I should ask Remy to show us his identity card. Remy was out of the house at the time as he had gone to buy oil for the lamps from a man in the street, but I noticed that he had left his coat hanging on the back of the kitchen door. His wallet was in one of the pockets, so I opened it to see if it contained his identity card. There didn't seem to be any harm in doing that and at least we would find out the truth about him. I was horrified when I found the brooch and ran in to show it to my husband's cousins. They advised me to put the wallet back in

Remy's pocket, to telephone the newspapers and then, once Monsieur Cros arrived and we had a witness, to confront Remy and make him produce the wallet. You know what happened after that.'

'I see, Madame,' Courtrand said stiffly, 'and may I ask why you summoned the press and not the police to be your witnesses?'

'You know very well why,' Josephine Hassler replied defensively. 'Because I believed that the police were no longer interested in the case and would do nothing.'

Courtrand pressed his lips together so that the corners of his mouth slanted downwards, a sign of extreme anger which Gautier recognized only too well. 'Perhaps, Madame, you do not realize who your real friends are.' He turned and faced Mansard. 'And you, Mansard, what do you have to say to this accusation?'

'It's false. Monsieur le Directeur! I swear it's false! I've never seen this brooch before and I know nothing of the robbery or the murders.'

'We shall see as to that. You will come with us to the headquarters of the Sûreté, where you will be questioned by the examining magistrate.'

'O, Holy Mother!' Mansard covered his face with his hands and began to cry. 'What will become of me?'

He was led away, escorted by police, to a horse-drawn police van which Courtrand had summoned by telephone and which was waiting outside the house. When they saw him being put into the van, the crowd gave an ironic cheer. This particular head did nothing to satisfy them.

'Leave the servants in peace!' a man shouted. 'And lock up the whore.'

'No chance of that,' someone yelled back. 'The president will see that she comes to no harm.'

When Courtrand and Gautier left the house a short time later several fists were shaken in their direction. Even this modest demonstration upset the director who was inordinately proud of what he supposed to be his universal popularity. His vanity blinded him to the truth which was that everyone knew his was a political appointment and accepted him because they accepted the system. Failed politicians, unsuccessful generals and the other misfits of public life had to be rewarded with a sinecure of an official post, if only to get them out of the way. Courtrand might be vain and pompous, but at least he was not dangerously incompetent or corrupt.

On the way back to Quai d'Orfèvres, he remarked to Gautier: 'Now at last we should get to know the truth. Mansard is the type who will break down under interrogation and tell everything.'

'That's assuming he really is implicated in this business.'

'There's not much doubt about that. You saw how he burst into tears.'

'If tears were a proof of guilt,' Gautier replied dryly, 'we would have to lock up every woman in France.'

IX

STARTING FROM THE couturier in Rue St Honoré which
Josephine Hassler had visited after leaving the Sûreté the previous
day, Gautier followed the route she had taken to the Rue Cambon
entrance of the Ritz. He found only one jeweller's shop on the way,
an establishment whose imposing, discreet façade told him that it
must be exclusive and forbiddingly expensive. Seeing it, he realized
that his thinking had been all wrong when he had sent policemen
knocking on the doors of dubious businesses which were known to
be not too fussy about what they bought. Josephine Hassler would
know nothing about that kind of shop and if she had jewelry to
conceal, what better place could there be than a fashionable
jeweller who catered only for ladies of society? The shop which
faced him now was exactly the type which she and her friends
would patronize.

Inside the shop a faded, middle-aged woman in a grey dress
was taking rings out of display cases and polishing them with a
chamois-leather. Gautier introduced himself, took from his pocket
the photograph of Josephine Hassler which he had found in the
official dossier of the case and showed it to the woman.

'This woman came into your shop yesterday, Madame. Can you
recall having seen her?'

The shop assistant looked at the photograph and then at Gautier
carefully. 'It would be better if you were to speak to my patron,
Monsieur Heuze.'

She opened a door at the back of the shop which led into a
small office, where a man sat at a desk checking entries in a leather-
bound accounts book. The jeweller's small imperial beard and long,
thin nose gave him an aristocratic air and he wore a heavy gold
watchchain looped across his waistcoat. When Gautier explained

the purpose of his visit, he closed the ledger deliberately and then adjusted the position of his watchchain. Gautier recognized the gesture as defensive, a retreat to a prepared position. In his experience people reacted in one of two ways when faced unexpectedly by the police: either they blustered aggressively or they took refuge in an attitude of injured innocence.

'It's unlikely that I would have seen this woman,' Heuze said, 'for clients are usually attended to by one of my two assistants; the lady to whom you have already spoken and a young man who has just gone to collect some pieces from our workshop.'

'A pity,' Gautier remarked. 'You would be a much more reliable witness, I'm sure. In my experience ladies like your assistant grow frightened and confused when they go before a magistrate.'

'Magistrate?' Heuze asked sharply. 'Are you suggesting that some offence has been committed in this establishment?'

'Not as far as I know, but the woman who visited your premises yesterday is involved in an important criminal matter. We are trying to trace certain items of missing jewelry.'

'Mine is not that sort of business!' Heuze said indignantly.

'I'm sure it isn't, but you must be prepared for some unfortunate publicity if the newspapers learn that one of your staff has appeared before the examining magistrate of this affair.'

'A number of very important and influential people are included among my clients, Inspector; royalty from more than one European country, for example.'

'So I understand.'

The jeweller was silent for a time, as though he were trying to decide how much of the truth he would have to tell in order to satisfy Gautier. Finally he said with great reluctance: 'The pearls were not stolen. When they were offered to me I made discreet enquiries both in Paris and abroad and it became clear that the necklace had been given to Madame Murat by a very important personality. So she was entirely within her rights to sell it.'

'Madame Murat?'

'Yes. She must, I assume, be the lady of whom you are making these enquiries.'

Gautier pushed the photograph of Josephine Hassler across the desk towards him. 'Is that her?'

61

'Yes, I believe so, although it's hard to be certain for she always wears a veil when she comes into the shop. She's been selling the pearls to me one or two at a time for some years now. They are a wonderful matched set and of course she would have got much more by selling the necklace as it was, but I understand she decided that this was not possible.'

'I didn't come here to make enquiries about a pearl necklace.'

'In that case I don't see how I can help you.'

'Perhaps you can, perhaps not.' Gautier handed Heuze a copy of the list of the jewelry which Josephine Hassler had reported as stolen. 'Did this Madame Murat, by any chance, ever bring you any pieces of jewelry that would fit the description of these? To clean, perhaps or possibly to repair?'

Heuze read through the list and then tapped the paper with his forefinger. 'These three rings could be the ones which she brought in last week.'

'To sell?'

'Certainly not! She wished to have the rings re-shaped and the stones set in a different form. I understand that she intends to give them to her daughter as a wedding present. The work is even now being carried out in our workshop.'

'And the other pieces?'

'I know nothing of these.' Heuze glanced down the list again. 'Except perhaps for the last item, the pearl brooch. That could be the brooch which Madame Murat brought in at the same time as her rings. It isn't a very good piece.'

'And is that also being reset?'

'No. That was why Madame Murat came in yesterday. She was going to have it re-made but she came to tell me she had changed her mind and wished to keep it as it was. I gather it had once belonged to her mother. She took the brooch away with her.'

Courtrand spoke scarcely a word to Gautier as they were being driven together to Impasse Louvain. Gautier could not remember having seen his chief so angry before and he suspected that at least part of the anger was aimed at himself, for having proved Courtrand wrong. It was true that at least the director had been spared the humiliation of having his mistake recorded in the files of the case because, by sheer chance, the examining magistrate Bertin had been engaged on other work that afternoon and Mansard had not been taken before him. So when Gautier had returned to the Sûreté with a signed statement from the jeweller, Heuze, about the pearl brooch, Courtrand had been able to release Mansard from custody without having actually arrested the manservant. Even so, Courtrand was very, very angry.

The afternoon was warm and sunny. In the sky above Invalides a balloon was drifting slowly towards the Eiffel Tower and from the basket festooned with bright ribbons which hung suspended beneath it, two people were waving to spectators below. In spite of the rumours that man was about to launch a flying machine heavier than air, ballooning was still a popular craze among Parisians and every day dukes, actresses and other eccentrics were lured up to sail above the roof-tops by a sense of adventure or by a desire for publicity.

They found Josephine Hassler sitting on the verandah of her house writing a letter, while her daughter sat nearby working on a piece of embroidery. When Gautier and Courtrand were admitted, Meg rose and without saying a word went into the house. The girl looked pale and tense.

'Ah, gentlemen!' Josephine Hassler said. 'You've come with good news, I hope. Has that scoundrel confessed?'

'The man whom you falsely accused, Madame,' Courtrand said icily, 'has been released and is no doubt on his way back here.'

'Why? What's happened?'

'We have a statement from a jeweller in Rue St Honoré that the brooch found in your servant's wallet was in your possession only yesterday.'

The colour drained slowly from Josephine Hassler's face except for two triangular patches of rouge above her cheekbones which, vivid against the pallor of her skin, gave her the appearance of an ageing doll. A faint moan came from her lips.

'We must conclude that your mother's brooch, if indeed it was hers, was not stolen on the night of the murders and that it was you who placed it in Mansard's wallet.' Josephine Hassler nodded, so Courtrand went on: 'And why did you do that may I ask?'

63

Instead of replying she began to sob. Although she bent her head, Gautier could see that her eyes remained dry but the sobs, great gasping convulsions, seemed genuine enough. The two men could do nothing but wait until her emotion abated and she was able to compose herself.

Eventually she said between sobs: 'How much longer must I endure this? You clearly do not comprehend what I am suffering; I, a girl brought up in kindness, gentleness and refinement. Do you know that when I came home yesterday the crowd outside the house jeered and mocked me? One woman even spat on me.'

Courtrand asked her patiently: 'Do you admit that you tried to incriminate an innocent man?'

'I admit putting the brooch in his wallet. Whether he's innocent or not only time will tell.'

'In the circumstances, Madame, I think it would be better if you were to make a statement under oath.'

X

MINISTRY OF JUSTICE

Crime at No. 8 Impasse Louvain   Dossier No. 0091

On this day, Wednesday, 11 June, we Gustave Courtrand, Commander of the Légion d'Honneur, Director General of the Sûreté, have heard on oath Josephine Hassler, who declared:

'It is true that I placed a brooch which I previously reported as having been stolen by those who murdered my husband and my mother, in the wallet of our servant, Remy Mansard, with the intention that this would be taken as evidence of his complicity in the murders. I saw no harm in this. For some time I had been suspicious of Remy, for it did not seem possible to me that he could have been in the house on the night of the murders and yet heard nothing. So many people had told me that the robbers must have had an accomplice in the household and everyone, even the newspapers, hinted that it must have been Remy. I began to believe them and soon I was convinced of his guilt. So I decided that if evidence of his complicity were found in his possession, he would break down and confess. He is, after all, a simple, uneducated creature and by nature timid. That is why I placed the brooch in his wallet.'

I then asked Madame Hassler why she had reported the brooch as having been stolen on the night of the crime. She stated:

'My mother had been wearing the brooch that evening, so naturally I assumed she would have left it on the table by her bed and that it must therefore have been stolen. However two or three days later I found it in my reticule and I remembered then that the clasp of the brooch had been faulty and as she thought it might fall off and be lost, my mother had given it to me for safekeeping. When I found it I took it to a jeweller to get the clasp repaired, meaning to inform the police when an opportunity arose.'

Madame Hassler was then told that the jeweller, Heuze, had stated that she had taken the brooch in and asked him to re-shape it and re-set the stones. She replied:

'Then he must have misunderstood me. It was the three rings that I wanted to have re-made. I took the rings to him at the same time, you know.'

When Madame Hassler was asked if these were not the three rings which she had also reported as stolen, she stated:

'No. They were similar, almost identical in fact, but not the same rings. You must understand that I owned these two sets of almost identical rings and I came to them in this way. A good friend of mine, a very important and influential person incidentally, wished to give me a present of jewels. I had been able to help and advise him in his business affairs and he merely wanted to show his gratitude. Imagine my difficulty! I could not of course be seen openly wearing jewels given to me by another man, for that would have been humiliating for my poor husband. So I had the idea of arranging for a set of rings to be made at the expense of my friend, that were as nearly as possible identical to those I already possessed. Thus I had two sets; one of rather ordinary rings which my husband had given me and the other mounted with extremely fine and valuable stones, the present of my friend. If anyone ever asked me why I had these two sets, I simply told them that one set of rings were just paste, made up as a precaution in case the originals should be stolen, which as you know is often done by women with good jewelry.'

I then asked Madame Hassler which of the two sets of rings had been stolen and why she had taken the remaining set to the jeweller and she replied:

'Fortunately the thieves took the less valuable rings and in fact I had the others locked away in a safe place. I decided that rather than risk anyone finding out the truth about the remaining rings, I would have them re-set in a different form and that when my daughter married I would give them to her as a wedding present.'

Madame Hassler was then asked if she wished to confirm her earlier statement that other pieces of jewelry had been stolen from her home on the night of the murders. She stated:

'Certainly. Do you imagine that I am in the habit of telling falsehoods? Three pieces of jewelry were taken from a drawer in my boudoir and your inspector has a description of them. I can understand why you are questioning me in this way. That rogue of a jeweller must have told you that I have been selling him my pearls and you are wondering what else I may have sold. The truth is that I have been short of money. Life is expensive in Paris and I have a salon to keep up, where many of the most prominent people in the city are to be found. That is the reason why I have had to sell the pearls which are my most valuable and my most precious jewels. And you, Monsieur Courtrand, know who is to blame for this state of affairs.'

At this point I reminded Madame Hassler that our enquiries were concerned only with the jewelry which she had reported as having been stolen and which might have been the motive for the break in at her house which had led to the murders. I asked her if there were anything more she wished to say on the matter of this jewelry and she stated:

'Nothing. All I can say is that I am truly sorry that I accused Remy Mansard who, it now appears, must be innocent. But you must remember, Monsieur Courtrand, and I wish this to be recorded for inclusion in the dossier of the case, that I have been suffering from an unbelievable strain, physical as well as mental. My doctor has been in attendance on me night and day and he is even now making me take ether and other drugs. You in the police have added to my suffering by your constant questioning and by your attitude of suspicion and hostility. In the circumstances it is not surprising that at times I may not be fully aware of what I am doing nor responsible for these actions.

> Statement recorded and signed by:
> Josephine Hassler
> Gustave Courtrand
> Jean-Paul Gautier

XI

RUE D'ORCHAMPT WAS a narrow street slanting upwards across the south side of the Butte in Montmartre. To reach it Gautier had to climb up from Place Blanche and cross Place Ravignan, a small cobbled square with a few trees and a couple of benches, on one of which a man in workman's overalls, who smelt strongly of wine, lay sleeping. It was in this square and on one of the benches, Gautier recalled, that during a particularly severe winter not long previously, an artist lurching home drunk one night from one of the many bistros in the neighbourhood, had stopped to rest, fallen asleep and been found the following morning dead from exposure.

Claudine Verdurin's name was written above a door on the second floor of number 4 Rue d'Orchampt. She took a long time to answer Gautier's knock and when she did open the door she was holding a bunch of dirty paint-brushes. Her hands were stained with paint and so was the old linen smock she was wearing.

'My policeman friend!' she exclaimed when she saw who the caller was. 'Don't tell me that I'm to be accused of another crime! The stabbing of that ponce whom they found dead not far from the Moulin Rouge last night, perhaps?'

Gautier grinned at the sarcasm. 'No. This time I've come to ask you for your help.'

'You must be demented! No one around here helps the police. Didn't you know that this is Montmartre, my friend: the home of thieves, pimps, prostitutes and artists?' She smiled unexpectedly. 'But still, you treated Eddie and me like human beings the other day, so I'll do the same for you. Come on in.'

She stepped aside to let him into the apartment. It consisted only of a single room and not a large one at that, sparsely furnished with a bed, a table, two chairs and an old tin trunk which had been partly covered with cushions. Several unframed canvasses hung on the walls and a newly-finished painting stood on an easel by the window. In one corner of the room there was an old-fashioned iron stove.

'I was cleaning my brushes,' Claudine explained and after drying the brushes in her hand with a piece of rag, she placed them in an empty jamjar.

'So you're an artist,' Gautier said, walking over towards the easel and looking at her painting.

'Let us say that I play at it, like one or two other women around here. But we don't get much encouragement.'

Gautier studied the painting which was a conventional study of a vase of flowers, executed with good draughtsmanship, although some might say that the colours were unnaturally vivid. He told Claudine: 'It's good.'

'Would you like to buy it?'

Her directness caught him off his guard. 'Policemen aren't supposed to buy paintings.'

'They do around here. So do landladies, shopkeepers, government clerks. In some bistros the owner will even take a picture in payment for a meal.'

'That doesn't sound like much of a deal for the artist. The canvas, the paint and all that labour for a two-franc meal?'

'It is when the artist hasn't eaten for a week.' Claudine picked up the flower painting and held it out at arm's length, looking at it critically. 'But this will cost you rather more, since I'm not exactly starving. Shall we say ten francs?'

'Right, I'll take it.' Even as he spoke, Gautier wondered at the impulse which had driven him to make this senseless gesture. It could only be a gesture, for the painting did not particularly attract him.

'You've made a good choice, Monsieur,' Claudine mocked him gently. 'The painting is wonderfully suited to a policeman's home. What would your family say if you took home one of these?'

She pointed towards the canvases on the walls. They were paintings in half-a-dozen different styles, all of them modern and plainly experimental; a group of people gathered around an infant's

70

cot all drawn in the flat two-dimensional outlines of primitive art; a woman in a ballet dress whose limbs and face were no more than a series of rectangular planes; a landscape in flaming reds and blues. Gautier was neither shocked nor surprised, for he had heard about the new breed of artists in Montmartre, their contempt for convention and their search for new art forms.

'Interesting. But I'll think I'll stick to my first choice.' He found a ten-franc piece in his pocket and handed it to Claudine.

'Excellent. And now that I'm in funds, I'll take you out to dinner.'

'You don't have to do that.'

'No, but I feel like it. Come on, we'll go to the Lapin.'

Gautier did not argue. He sensed that Claudine herself might not have eaten too recently and that the money he had just given her might be all she possessed. Many other girls would probably have scrounged a meal from him, but by selling him a painting she both got the meal and kept her independence. For a reason that he could not identify, he felt flattered.

Leaving the apartment, they walked up the hill and through the Place du Tertre. It was early evening and most of the bistros were already full. As daylight faded, artists abandoned their studios and went in search of company, preferring to spend what money they had on drink rather than on oil lamps which would give them light to go on working. Later the night would liven up with singing inside the cabarets and outside a few drunks yelling or swearing or fighting.

The Lapin Agile was in Rue des Saules on the far side of the Butte. Facing it was a small vineyard, a relic of the days when the whole hillside was covered in vines and not far away lay the Maquis, an area almost overgrown with scrawny trees, shrubs and weeds and dotted with shacks in which lived ragmen, pedlars, and more than a few cut-throats. Originally the building had been a shooting lodge, constructed by Henry IV and conveniently placed by the home of one of his mistresses. When it was converted into a cabaret, the artist André Gill, asked to paint a sign for it, had produced one showing a rabbit escaping from a casserole, so it became the Lapin A Gill, soon corrupted to the Lapin Agile.

When they were seated at a table outside the cabaret, with a litre of red wine between them, waiting for the meal they had ordered, Claudine said: Haven't you forgotten something?'

'What?'

'The reason why you came to see me this evening.'

He smiled because it was true. 'That's the effect you have on a man.'

She pulled a face. 'I shall take that for a compliment; a policeman's compliment.'

'I wanted to talk to you about Félix Hassler. You modelled for him didn't you?'

'Only for a very short time and that was long ago. What do you want to know?'

'Anything. Everything. As you've probably guessed we're making no progress in this case at all. We've questioned everyone who might in any way be connected with it. We've got a dossier full of statements. Everyone has plenty to say. The Hassler woman has told us enough about herself to fill a book, but she has never mentioned her husband. If we knew what sort of man he was, it might give us an idea of why anyone might wish to kill him.'

Claudine thought about this for a time, eating the terrine which they had ordered and which had now been served. Watching her, Gautier was struck by the delicacy of her features. Although her face, as he had noticed before, had the look of a cheeky urchin, its contours, the cheekbones, the nose, mouth and chin had the fine lines that most people would regard as a sign of aristocratic birth. She was wearing the same shapeless dress that she had worn when he last saw her and her hair hung to her shoulders in a way which suggested that she took little interest in her appearance. Gautier found himself wondering what she would look like dressed in the high fashion of the day, with a high-waisted dress, a hat, long gloves and jewelry. She might easily be beautiful.

'In a way I felt sorry for Félix Hassler,' she said finally, 'He used to be a painter of stained-glass windows, you know, and I believe he would have been happier if he had stuck to that. Painting portraits is one of the most exacting branches of art and to be frank, he didn't have the talent for it. When I sat for him he used to talk about the old days and how when he worked in those damp, chilly cathedrals he used to wear under his smock to keep him warm, a long knitted cardigan right down to his knees. He enjoyed the practical side of his work, climbing up scaffolding, taking measurements, talking to workmen. On the other hand he never appeared to take much pride in the portraits he had painted. I suspect that his wife used her influence to get him commissions.'

'Influence is not exactly the right word. She used to sleep with rich men and they paid her in portraits.'

'That doesn't surprise me. You know that he painted a portrait of the late president?'

'So I understand.'

'When I asked Félix about it and what sort of man the president was, he said very little. Poor Félix!' Claudine shook her head and tore a piece from the bread beside her plate as though the memory of the painter's humiliation irritated her. 'Men! She treated him like that and yet he was content to be completely dependent on her.'

'Perhaps he had a mistress.'

'Not a chance. When I first went to sit for him, he made advances in a timid kind of way. He wasn't really interested in me and I'm sure he only did it because he knew artists are supposed to make a pass at their models.'

'Could he have been jealous of his wife, do you think?'

'Possibly, but he would never have made a scene about her behaviour or been violent to her, if that's what you're thinking. He was rather droll about his wife in a pathetic kind of way. Once when I was sitting for him, he saw a man hanging around in the lane outside their house and grew quite agitated. Apparently he had seen the man there before. What worried him, would you believe it, was that his wife might see the man and think he was having her watched by detectives.'

Gautier thought about what she had told him and then asked her: 'Can you remember if there was anyone else in the house at the time? Any visitors?'

'Yes. His wife was entertaining some man; an important man I believe. I remember thinking that if the man outside in the lane was a detective, then he was more likely to be working for the wife of the man downstairs, but I didn't want to hurt Hassler by saying so.'

Gautier was beginning to realize that Claudine's determination to prove her independence and her sometimes aggressive sense of humour were only a façade behind which lay qualities of sympathy and kindness. She reminded him in some ways of Monique, a little dressmaker's assistant who had been his mistress for almost two years. Though she was much less intelligent than Claudine, Monique had liked to think of herself as sophisticated, but often when they were alone, her innocence and credulity had shown through. Almost the only domestic problem which she had caused him was on the night of 31 December 1899, when she had insisted that he had spent the night with her, because she was convinced that the world was going to end with the millenium at midnight. When midnight passed and nothing happened, she had been furious with Gautier.

Dragging himself back from the past he asked Claudine: 'Did you by any chance see the man who was waiting outside Hassler's house that day?'

'Yes, I did. Félix was so anxious that he made me go to the window to look at the fellow. He wanted to know if I thought he looked like a detective, though how I was supposed to know that God knows.'

'Can you remember what he looked like?'

'Nondescript really, but he was stylishly dressed for a detective: long belted overcoat, a brown Derby hat and spats.'

'Would you recognize him if you saw him again?'

'I well might. He was not far from the house and looked up at Félix and me quite openly. Clearly he wasn't worried about whether anybody saw him there or not.'

Claudine could remember nothing more about the Hassler household which would have been worth telling Gautier. So they finished their meal and lingered over another bottle of wine. He learned that her mother had been a circus rider at the Nouveau Cirque. Lady riders in the many circuses in Paris were usually beautiful and much admired by clubmen. They could earn as much as 10,000 francs in a year and the famous Nouveau Cirque near Place Vendôme was the most chic in Paris. Claudine's father, she told him, had been the youngest son of a duke and her mother, returning too soon to the circus after her pregnancy, had fallen from her horse and broken her hip so badly that she could never perform again.

'She got a job selling vegetables in the Halles,' Claudine added.

'Surely your father made provision for her?'

'I like to think that he would have done but the duchess his mother, afraid that he might even marry my mother, packed him off to Africa before I was born. He died out there of dysentery not long afterwards.'

'And your mother?'

'We managed all right. Then two years ago she caught a sudden pneumonia and died.'

They walked back to her apartment together. Claudine had insisted on paying for the dinner. It cost only four francs, wine included, and she told him laughingly that there would still be enough left of the price he had paid for her painting to let her eat for three more days. Gautier could not decide whether she was being serious or not.

'You've helped me,' he said abruptly, half afraid that his next remark would be misunderstood, yet meaning it. 'And I'd like to do something for you in return.'

'If you feel like that you can,' she replied, surprising him once again.

'What?'

'Let me paint you.'

They had reached the house where she lived and stopped outside the door. He laughed. 'You can't possibly be serious.'

'Of course I am. You have an interesting face, craggy and masculine, but interesting. Anyway I can't afford a professional model.'

He laughed again, still believing she was mocking him. Raising one hand she traced with her finger the line of his face from cheek to chin.

'It won't mean many sittings,' she said persuasively, 'for I work very fast. Come just whenever you feel like it.'

XII

SURAT'S TRIP TO the region of Beaucourt and Montbéliard was far more productive than he had expected. When he returned to Paris his pessimism had disappeared and he came into Gautier's office with all his former enthusiasm. First of all he told Gautier what he had found out about the man with whom Josephine Hassler had lunched at the Ritz Hotel.

Colonel Gerard de Clermont it appeared, resided in the Château d'Ivry, just over ten kilometres to the south-west of Beaucourt. He was descended from a minor branch of the Clermont-Polignac family, one of France's oldest and most aristocratic dynasties. His parents, however, had been far from rich and unable to maintain more than a modest household on their country estate at Fontainebleau or in their Paris apartment. Since Gerard was the third of seven sons, it had been decided that he must enter the army and after training at St Cyr, he had been commissioned in the Hussars. In his early 30's he had left the army, some said he had been forced to resign after a scandal, and shortly afterwards he had married the Comtesse de Balincourt, a widow with three daughters, sixteen years older than de Clermont and the owner through inheritance from her husband of the Château d'Ivry.

Herself the daughter of an industrialist from Rouen, Madame de Balincourt had been wealthy in her own right and it had been her money that had paid for the restoration and upkeep of the Château d'Ivry. After his marriage to the comtesse, Colonel de Clermont lived the life of a country landowner and about three years previously his wife had died. Since that time two of his stepdaughters had married, leaving the youngest to live at the château and keep house for the colonel.

'What do the locals feel about this colonel?' Gautier asked Surat.

76

'He's not popular, even though he's obviously wealthy and lives in style, which must be good for the local tradespeople. But they complain that he's arrogant and ill-tempered and treats his servants badly, sometimes violently.'

'Any scandals?'

None. He seems to be a man of high moral rectitude and a regular church-goer. On the other hand he pays frequent visits to Paris and the gossips hint that the motive for these is a woman.'

'What's your opinion?'

Surat shrugged his shoulders. 'It's hard to say. He's a member of the Cercle Agricole which could be a reason for coming to Paris.'

'To play cards with his fellow clubmen? Could be, I suppose.'

'While I was down there I did a little research at the local newspaper office,' Surat said, 'and I found out something which will interest you much more than Colonel de Clermont.'

He took a wallet from the breast-pocket of his jacket and from it produced a newspaper cutting. Before he could hand it to Gautier, they were interrupted as Courtrand burst into the room. Only on rare occasions did the director visit the offices of any of his subordinates and it was usually a sign that he was displeased. Today was no exception.

'Is it true that you sent Surat down to the village where Madame Hassler was born?' he asked Gautier angrily.

'Yes, at least to that region. I wanted him to make enquiries about a man who she has been meeting secretly.'

'Are you deliberately flouting my authority?' So great was his rage that Courtrand had difficulty in standing still.

'Of course not.'

'I have already made a public declaration that Madame Hassler is not implicated in the murders in any way. What are people going to think if it is known that we are still trying to find evidence that would link her with the crimes? That I am a liar? Or simply that I don't know what's going on in my department? It's intolerable.'

'I felt we should continue to explore every possibility,' Gautier said, 'until we find one piece of real evidence.'

'Are you stupid?' Courtrand ranted on, ignoring what Gautier had said. 'Do you really believe that a woman like Madame

77

Hassler, educated, cultured, respected, would kill her own mother? You're as bad as the newspapers!'

'I'm only saying that her story is impossible to believe.'

'The decision to believe or not to believe does not rest with you, Gautier. Kindly stop wasting the time and money of my department and confine your investigations to those matters on which I direct you.'

He left the room as noisily as he had entered it. Gautier felt a hot surge of anger as he watched him go. To be rebuked in such tones in front of a subordinate was humiliating enough, but he resented still more the injustice of the rebuke. Courtrand was not an idiot and he must be fully aware that Josephine Hassler's account of what had happened at Impasse Louvain was flimsy and wholly improbable. The Sûreté, if it were to carry out its duty, must search for evidence that would either confirm her story or destroy it. If Courtrand wished to sweep the whole affair under the carpet, then he should have been honest and told Gautier so.

'What's eating the old man?' Surat asked when the two of them were alone.

'The press has been having a go at him. They're hinting that he used to be one of the Hassler woman's lovers and that's why he's trying to cover up for her.'

'Perhaps you should have shown him this.'

Surat handed Gautier the newspaper clipping he was holding and which he had been going to give him when Courtrand interrupted them. It was a report cut from a regional paper dated more than twenty years previously. Gautier read it through once and then a second time, thoughtfully.

'No, I think it might be better if we didn't make this public,' he said.

Surat looked stunned. 'Are you saying we should ignore it?'

'Not at all. What I said was that we shouldn't make it public. Perhaps someone else could do the job for us—and better. Leave the cutting with me.'

After Surat had left his office, Gautier telephoned *Figaro*. He was told that Duthrey had not arrived at his desk but was expected at any moment, so he left a message asking the journalist to meet him at the Café Corneille as soon as he could manage it.

The day was warm and sunny, so he walked to the Corneille and arriving there found a table on the pavement outside. Thinking that it was too early in the day for an absinthe or an aperitif, he ordered a glass of Alsatian beer and as he sipped it thought about what Surat had told him that morning. Wealthy, aristocratic, arrogant, fastidious, Colonel de Clermont seemed to him exactly the type of man who would appeal to Josephine Hassler. Gautier would have liked to know more about the colonel, to dig more deeply into their relationship, but to do so would mean defying Courtrand's instructions. So long as Courtrand was determined to keep the lid tightly down on the Impasse Louvain affair, nothing could be done. He had already decided that Courtrand's hand must be forced and the lid lifted.

When Duthrey arrived at the café, Gautier did not waste time on civilities. He said to the journalist: 'You asked me the last time we met to let you know if you could ever do me a favour.'

'What is it?'

He handed Duthrey the newspaper report that Surat had given him. 'One of my men came across this in Montbéliard. It's a clipping from the *Voix de L'Est* of a story which the paper printed in 1881. You know, of course, that Josephine Hassler was born and brought up not far from Montbéliard. It would be quite helpful if you could use this clipping in your own distinctive way.'

Duthrey read the report through and when he had finished whistled in astonishment. 'Use it? My God, with this I can lift the roof right off the Ministry of Justice!'

Reading Duthrey's piece in *Figaro* next morning added enormously to Gautier's enjoyment of a breakfast already pleasurable for being leisurely and late. It was his turn for a late duty at the Sûreté that day, starting at noon, and although in the normal way when he was working on a major case, he did not bother about the hours he worked, this time he had decided to follow the rules. By doing so he would avoid being at the Sûreté when Duthrey's story broke and when ministers, prefects and judges began to show their wrath. After so many scandals in recent years – a president's son-in-law selling decorations, a minister of education having little girls pro-cured for him, the Panama swindle – people in high places had become extremely sensitive to newspaper attacks. Keeping out of the way was not moral cowardice on the part of Gautier, but a modest piece of revenge. Courtrand had been protecting Josephine Hassler; let him be there when the storm broke.

He read through Duthrey's article again:

THE MURDERS AT IMPASSE LOUVAIN

Who Will Believe Josephine Hassler Now?

Little progress has so far been made by the authorities in solving the riddles which surround the infamous murders at Impasse Louvain. Many of our readers have been wondering why. Was it because that gentle magistrate, Bertin, when examining the beautiful Josephine spent too much time in reminiscing about the cultured evenings he had spent in her salon? Was it perhaps that the chief of the Sûreté, Gustave Courtrand, was so seduced by the charm of Josephine that he preferred basking in the soft glances of her dark eyes to following the trail of the murderers? Could it have been that the two of them actually believed the fantastic story Madame Hassler had told about that fateful night, that they believed in the bearded men and the long cloaks and the lanterns?

When in the past this newspaper has declared that Madame Hassler's story was unbelievable we have been accused of cynicism. Magistrates, police, even a section of our readers have spoken up in her defence. 'What she says must be true,' they cried, 'for no one could possibly have invented such an unlikely story.'

Today we have another story to tell; a story which took place in the town of Montbéliard more than twenty years ago; a story reported in the local newspaper at the time, which we have verified as true from police records.

One night in April 1878 the peace of Montbéliard was rudely shattered when the door of a house in the centre of the town burst open and a maidservant rushed out into the street shouting for help. Those who went to her assistance found in the house an elderly schoolmaster and his wife bound to their beds by their wrists and ankles, their mouths gagged with cottonwool. When released, the couple said they had been attacked in their beds by intruders, two men with red beards and a monstrously ugly woman, all of them wearing long cloaks and carrying lanterns and pistols. The schoolmaster's wife declared that her life had been threatened and that she had been forced to tell the robbers where the key to the strongbox in which they kept their savings was hidden.

Despite extensive searches and enquiries, the police were unable to find any trace of the supposed intruders and eventually they abandoned their efforts and the case was closed. It was only years later when the schoolmaster died that his wife came forward and admitted that the whole affair had been deliberately staged by her husband and herself in order to cover up the fact that they had embezzled some school funds with which they had been entrusted.

We scarcely need to remind our readers that Josephine Hassler spent her girlhood at Beaucourt, less than an hour's journey from Montbéliard. At the time when these events took place she travelled regularly to Montbéliard for lessons in the pianoforte and in dancing. Moreover her maternal grandparents as it happens kept the Red Lion inn which is situated in the same street as the house in which the schoolmaster lived and only a very short distance away.

And today what are we to believe? That Josephine Hassler never heard of this bogus robbery which, in a town as small as Montbéliard must have created a sensation? That she did not hear about the red beards, the long black cloaks, the cottonwool gags? That she was not aware that in spite of all their efforts the police in Montbéliard were unable to prove what really had happened? If we believe this then we may even believe that the events she has described really did happen in Impasse Louvain and that she is just the victim of a coincidence even more bizarre than her own story.

We must leave our readers to judge for themselves, since it is too much to expect that Judge Bertin and Director Courtrand would be so ungallant as to question the honesty of such a seductive lady.

Gautier put down the newspaper and finished his croissant. Suzanne was sitting facing him across the table, holding her cup of coffee in both hands, blowing on it gently. Not for the first time he noticed that although she was not quite 30, she was beginning to show signs of impending middle-age. Physically she had scarcely changed, her face had retained its almost childish prettiness and there was none of that fleshiness around her waist and buttocks which in a woman often marks the final departure of youth. It was her gestures and her attitudes, the way she was holding her cup, the way she pulled her dressing-gown tightly around her, which showed that subconsciously she was moving towards the comfort and repose of middle-age.

He remembered Claudine when she sat facing him across another table not so long ago. Eager, combative, ready for any challenge, Claudine was a generation apart from Suzanne. Was this, he thought, the reason why men were unfaithful? A sudden realization not that they had outgrown their wives, but that their wives had grown older than them.

Putting the thought out of his mind, he finished his breakfast and set out for the Sûreté. When he arrived, a messenger was waiting inside the entrance to tell him that Courtrand required his presence urgently. He went up to the director's office on the first floor, prepared for a major row but also ready to enjoy it, knowing now that right was on his side.

Courtrand was at his desk, signing a pile of reports that represented the work of the previous day on a score of crimes. He kept Gautier waiting until he had finished and then looked up at him calmly.

'You've seen the article in *Figaro,* I suppose?'

'Yes.'

'A pity we had to allow the newspapers to make this important discovery. Surat could have more usefully spent his time in the local newspaper office in Montbéliard, than chasing around after some superannuated colonel.'

Gautier wanted to burst out laughing in admiration. Bloody little bantam cock, he thought, there's simply no way of repressing him. Cheek, bombast and a thick skin, that's what one needed to be Director of the Sûreté.

'I've been waiting for you,' Courtrand said, like a king bestowing the accolade of knighthood, 'because you should be present when I speak to Madame Hassler.'

'You've sent for her then?'

'She's already here, waiting in another room. Just tell my assistant to go and fetch her, will you?'

Gautier relayed this message to the director's personal assistant who worked in an adjoining office not much larger than a cupboard. Josephine must have been waiting not too far away because after only a few seconds she was ushered into Courtrand's office. As on the last occasion when Gautier had seen her, she was dressed completely in black, but he noticed that now she was wearing a different veil, a superb piece of Brussels lace which showed enough of her features to provoke admiration rather than sympathy.

Courtrand came straight to the point. He said: 'Have you by any chance read *Figaro* this morning, Madame?'

'Certainly not! I refuse to read a paper that has constantly been defaming me.'

'Then perhaps, Madame, you should listen while I read this article to you.'

Slowly and precisely he read the whole of Duthrey's article aloud, determined, it seemed, that she should hear and understand every innuendo. Josephine Hassler had lifted her veil when she sat down and Gautier watched her as Courtrand was reading. A twitching of the lips was the first sign of emotion which she showed and then slowly her face took on a hunted expression. She closed her eyes, either to conceal the fear which showed in them or to help her concentrate as her mind raced wildly, searching for an escape.

'Well, Madame,' Courtrand said, putting down the newspaper, 'And what have you to say to that?'

'It's untrue,' Josephine Hassler whispered and Gautier could see that she was trembling.

'What is untrue? The story you told us about the night your husband and your mother were murdered?'

'No, what the newspaper says. They've invented the story about Montbéliard to trick me into an admission.'

'No, Madame. What they say has been checked with police files. The incident at Montbéliard took place exactly as they describe it.'

83

'In that case I know nothing about it. Why should I have heard of it? I was only a child at the time.'

'You must have been all of eighteen.'

'At that age I never read newspapers. My father believed that we children should be educated in a civilized and cultured way, reading only the best books, learning music, art and deportment. He used to tell me that newspapers were full of lies and scandals and totally unfit for young girls of refinement.'

'Ah, yes,' Courtrand said with cruel sarcasm. 'And I suppose your grandparents, the innkeepers, would have been too refined to talk about the affair even though it happened in their street and caused a sensation in the town?'

'I can only repeat that I heard nothing of it,' Josephine Hassler said and there was a note of despair in her stubbornness.

'The examining magistrate will decide whether you are to be believed.'

'Monsieur Bertin knows I am incapable of lying.'

'Bertin is no longer responsible for this case,' Courtrand said brusquely. 'Because of the articles in the press he has been relieved and Loubet is taking charge.'

'Is this a conspiracy?' Josephine Hassler asked. 'Am I to be hounded not only by the papers and the public but by the police and Ministry of Justice as well?' She rose to her feet, drawing the threadbare vestiges of her dignity around her. 'I can see no reason why I must endure your slanders and your questions any longer.'

Courtrand held up one hand. 'Wait, Madame, until you have heard the rest of what I have to say.'

She sat down again. 'And what is that?'

'It concerns the rings which you reported as stolen.'

'I have explained about the rings.'

'You told us that you had two sets and that the ones which were stolen were those your husband had given you.'

'That's right.'

'Regrettably we know that statement to be false, Madame. What you did not realize is that every piece of jewelry has a mark by which it can be recognized and all jewellers are required to keep a register of every piece they make and sell. We have checked the records and established that the rings which you took in to be

84

re-shaped were those your husband gave you. Why not admit that there was no duplicate set of rings and that no jewelry was stolen from your house on the night of the murders?'

Gautier thought that Josephine Hassler was going to faint. She turned very pale, shivered and her head slumped forward so that she was staring at her gloved hands. Finally, she said hoarsely: 'I did have other jewels, presents from a friend, but I had to sell them just as I had to sell the pearls.'

'We are not talking of pearls.'

'You, the authorities, the government, you drove me to it,' she continued, ignoring Courtrand's remark.

'Drove you to what? Murder?'

'They promised me 500,000 francs. You know that Monsieur Courtrand. But all I received was 100,000. They broke faith with me after imploring me to be silent.'

Courtrand glanced at Gautier uneasily as he said: 'This is not the time to talk about that other matter, Madame.'

'Why should I remain silent any longer?' Josephine Hassler demanded, her voice suddenly shrill with nervous agitation. 'It was the government who broke their word and so reduced me to selling the pearls. I have expenses, Monsieur, an exclusive salon to maintain, a daughter to marry.'

'When the government promised to recompense you for your services to the late president, they did not realize that you were in possession of a necklace which the donor had no right to give you. Otherwise they would not have made you such a generous offer.'

In spite of the way in which Courtrand had phrased his reply, Gautier knew now that the rumour which had swept Paris after the death of the late president must have been true. Josephine Hassler had been his mistress, she had been present when he had died and she had been bribed to keep silent.

'And what good was the necklace, may I ask?' she continued. 'Because of the scandal I was never able to wear it.'

'If you had given it back as you were advised, you would have received the balance of the sum which you had been promised.'

'What! A mere 400,000 francs? It's worth five times as much!'

Courtrand was having difficulty in restraining his temper and he began to shout. 'You would do better to hold your tongue, Madame.

Had you not spoken so freely to the newspapers, had you not made false accusations, had you not lied so often, you would not be in this position.'

'Attacked by the press, badgered by the police, spat on in the streets, how could my position be worse? Tell me that, Monsieur Courtrand.'

Opening a drawer in his desk, Courtrand took out very slowly and theatrically, a sheet of blue paper. He said in solemn, pompous tones: 'I have to tell you Madame Josephine Hassler, that it has been decided you are to be indicted. My instructions are that you must be arrested.'

Josephine Hassler looked at him incredulously. 'Arrested? Are you saying that I'm to be put in prison?'

'Console yourself Madame, with the thought that in prison you will be safe; safe from the crowds who would like to lynch you and even more important, safe from your own indiscretions.'

'Never!' Josephine Hassler leapt to her feet as she shouted: 'Do you imagine I'm to be put away like any dumb little prostitute, when I cause you trouble? You'll never silence me! The world will know everything!'

Courtrand stood up to face her. For a small man he could command dignity and authority even when, as now, he was obviously enjoying the scene. 'You may make your choice, Madame. If you persist in this hysteria I shall have you conveyed to an asylum for the criminally deranged.'

For a long minute Josephine Hassler was silent. Then she asked: 'And the alternative?'

'St Lazare prison.'

XIII

FROM A SHOP in one of the narrow streets around Montmartre, Gautier bought a bottle of red wine.He realized that not wishing to arrive at anyone's house empty-handed was a typically bourgeois attitude and one which the bohemians of the Butte would scorn, but even so he had decided he must take something when he went to call on Claudine. This would be a way of showing her that he was coming on a social and not a professional visit. He had chosen wine only after much thought – a gift of food might be resented, flowers misconstrued – and the choice of the wine itself had needed careful deliberation for an expensive wine would be ostentation, a vin ordinaire patronizing.

When Claudine opened the door to his knock and he handed her the bottle she said, though not unkindly: 'Only a policeman would have brought wine. Have you no romance in you? Why not flowers?'

'Well, I couldn't share flowers with you, could I?'

'Then you may drink your share while I begin sketching. You have come to pose for me, haven't you?'

'If you insist.'

She arranged her easel near the window where she would get the last of the early evening light and made him sit on a chair at a table carefully placed so that she could draw him in profile. Then setting the wine bottle and a glass on the table in front of him, she took a stick of charcoal and began sketching with swift, easy strokes.

'How is the Hassler woman?' she asked as she worked. 'Has she found any more bearded men?'

'You must be the only person in Paris who doesn't know she's in prison.'

87

'As I told you, I don't read newspapers. Is she going to be tried for the two murders?'

'Not necessarily. She will be examined by the magistrate in charge of the case and on the basis of his findings it will be decided whether she should be put on trial.'

'Does that mean you've finished working on the case?'

'My God, no! Far from it! Loubet, the magistrate, is ordering numerous investigations to be made before he will even start examining the Hassler woman. All the enquiries we've made so far have to be checked and formal statements taken. We're looking for more witnesses and for people who can be questioned on the woman's character and past life; even people who knew her as a girl, neighbours, governesses, schoolfriends are being sought out and asked to testify. Two more inspectors have been assigned to help me on the case and even so we've far too much to do. It's a policeman's worst nightmare!'

'How long will the examination take?'

Gautier explained that in complex criminal cases the 'instruction' as it was called, could stretch out over several weeks. Throughout this period a member of the Sûreté would have to collect the prisoner from prison each day and escort her to the Palais de Justice. Then, if she were put on trial, Gautier would almost certainly be required to give evidence.

'This is bound to be a long and tedious business,' he said. 'Why, already the official dossier runs into more than 100 pages and we have scarcely begun.'

'Do I read in the tone of your voice that you think it'll all be a waste of time?'

'It could be,' Gautier said cautiously, not wishing to expose his real views.

'So you don't believe that Josephine Hassler is guilty?'

'I believe that if she is put on trial, she'll be acquitted.'

'That doesn't answer my question.'

'If you're asking whether I think she murdered her husband, then the answer is No. On the other hand I refuse to believe the story she has been telling about what happened that night in her house. We might be able to convince a jury that she was lying, but that wouldn't prove she was guilty of murder.'

88

'But it would make her an accomplice, at least?'

'Yes, I believe so.'

Putting down the stick of charcoal, Claudine wiped her hands on a piece of rag, found another glass and came over to the table to fill it with wine. While she drank, she stood leaning on the sill of the open window. The only view it offered was one of a narrow back yard, piled high with discarded furniture and beyond that a sea of chimneys. She glanced out briefly and then turned to look at Gautier.

'If it won't offend your professional integrity,' she said with no more than a trace of sarcasm, 'tell me who you think killed those people at Impasse Louvain.'

'At this moment I have no idea. Josephine Hassler knows of course, but she'll never tell us. She's stubborn as well as cunning, that one. Personally I wonder whether blackmail may not be at the bottom of it.'

'Blackmail? How?'

'Again I really don't know, but the Hassler woman was in the classic position to be either blackmailed or blackmailer. For a start there was this business about the death of the late president. For how long and how deeply had he compromised himself with her? She makes some vague claim to having important papers. Was he idiot enough to let her get her hands on State papers? At a much lower level, how much did her husband know about her adulteries? He might well even have been in league with her in some extortion racket. Or again might not some servant or hotel porter have been blackmailing her? She's not the kind of woman who would take very kindly to the humiliation of a divorce scandal.'

'Adultery, divorce, blackmail!' Claudine exclaimed scornfully. 'They all spring from society's ridiculous attitude to marriage.'

'Don't say you're opposed to marriage.'

'Not at all; only to the one-sided marriages we have in France today. A man can have as many mistresses as he likes or spend every night in a brothel, but if a woman steps out of line only once, she's branded as an adulteress and dragged into the divorce courts. What is worse is that under the law she has no rights.'

Gautier laughed. 'You're a feminist! I suppose you belong to the Society for the rights of Women?'

'I do indeed. Why should there be one law for men and another for women. Tell me that. After all you're a policeman.'

'We enforce the law, we don't make it.'

Claudine made a disparaging noise, put her empty glass down on the table and returned to the easel. Soon she was sketching again, but that did not stop her giving Gautier a short lecture on a subject that obviously stirred her indignation, the inequality of the sexes. She reminded him of the old French saying that there were only two occupations for a woman, wife or cocotte, and that those women who did work as sempstresses or making hats or artificial flowers were scandalously underpaid, earning on the average between ten and twenty centimes an hour. She reminded him too that a husband had a right to half of any money which his wife might earn.

Gautier had heard all the arguments before, for as a young policeman he had more than once been on duty at public meetings when militant feminists like Louise Michel, the 'Red Virgin', had demanded equal rights for women. He did not mind the lecture because he enjoyed watching the animation in Claudine's face and hearing the indignation in her voice.

'All what you say may well be true,' he said whe: she had finished, 'but at least under criminal law men and women get the same treatment.'

'Rubbish! A man who beats up another man is arrested; if he thrashes a woman, you look the other way.'

'No, I won't accept that.'

'I can give you an example. A girl named Mimi who lives in the same building as Eddie York, is a hostess in some establishment in Rue des Moulins.'

'Did you say a hostess? Those places in Rue des Moulins are nothing more than high-class brothels.'

'Well, whatever she does, not long ago she was brutally assaulted by some man in the place who went berserk. She finished up in hospital with two broken ribs, a fractured cheekbone and internal injuries. If another man hadn't intervened she would have been killed. And yet the man who attacked her wasn't arrested.'

'Were the police called?'

'Yes, but they did nothing.'

'Perhaps the girl wouldn't make a complaint. Those places are not keen on getting involved with the flics in any way. It's bad for their business.'

'If that's true it's a scandal!'

Gautier decided it would be tactful to change the subject. 'By the way,' he remarked, 'how is your friend York?'

'He has left Paris and gone to live in St Tropez.'

'Did we frighten him away?'

'Possibly. Eddie's the type who turns pale even when he sees a policeman. But the real attraction in St Tropez is a boyfriend, this Spanish painter, I forget his name. Eddie's a pede, you know.'

'A homosexual? I thought you and he—'

'You were wrong.' She interrupted him firmly. 'It's just like the police to jump to conclusions. I used to pose for Eddie, that's all.'

'Have some more wine,' Gautier said placatingly, 'At least we can make sure that this bottle is divided equally between the sexes.'

He poured out the wine, took her glass over to her and stood watching as she worked on her sketch, smudging along the lines she had made with the charcoal with one finger to give a shading effect. Although the drawing was a fair likeness, no one could possibly have described it as great art. Gautier decided charitably that Claudine was probably experimenting, trying for an effect for which her technique was not yet sufficiently proficient.

'This is only to get the feel of your face and its bone structure,' she explained as though she had read his thoughts. 'I'll need to do two or three more of these and then I'll start work in oils. That will be something quite different, not so much a portrait as a study.' She looked at the sketch and then at Gautier's face critically. 'I might even try my hand at cubism. That might work well with those flat rectangular planes of your face.'

'And with my flat head, I suppose.'

She laughed. 'Now you know what it's like to be an artist's model. The hours are long, the pay is bad and the result is never flattering.'

'I could accept all that, but I'm disappointed about one thing.

'What's that?'

'Didn't you tell me that artists were expected to make advances to their models?'

'Only male artists.'

'There you are,' Gautier complained. 'You want the same rights as a man but you shirk the obligations.'

XIV

THE JUDICIAL examination of Josephine Hassler was, as Gautier had predicted, prolonged over several weeks. On the days when the magistrate, Loubet, summoned her for questioning, Gautier and another inspector went to St Lazare prison and took her in a carriage to the Palais de Justice. They were armed with revolvers, not to stop the prisoner escaping, but because the authorities were fearful of public demonstrations against her. The Impasse Louvain affair had aroused a surprising amount of public feeling and whenever Josephine Hassler was taken from or to St Lazare, crowds gathered to jeer and shout at her. There had even been some talk of a lynching.

At the Palais de Justice, the inspectors took Josephine Hassler, invariably after a long wait of an hour or more, to the office of Loubet. There she was joined by her counsel, Mâitre Bonnard, one of the best-known and most highly-paid criminal lawyers in France. The procedure of examination was simple. Loubet sat on one side of a long table with the documents and notes on the case spread out in front of him. At one end of the table sat his clerk who had the duty of noting the magistrate's questions and the prisoner's answers and of preparing at the end of each session, a record of the proceedings which had to be signed as correct by all three of them. Josephine Hassler was placed at the other end of the table, which by chance and design, faced the windows so that a searching light fell across her face. The two inspectors and Mâitre Bonnard sat behind the magistrate, dumb witnesses, because they played no active part in the examination.

Throughout the period of the instruction, Josephine Hassler wore the same clothes, a long, loose black dress, a black cloak and low-heeled shoes. The very simplicity of the clothes and the pallor

93

of her face, totally devoid of cosmetics, made her seem to Gautier even more beautiful than usual, with an air of martyred innocence.

On the day following each session of the interrogation he would receive a copy of the proceedings. These he was supposed to read through so that he could, if required, report to Courtrand on how the case was developing. This rarely happened as the Director of the Sûreté appeared to have lost all interest in the Impasse Louvain affair. The pattern of the examination did not vary much from day to day and Loubet's strategy was evidently to question the prisoner repeatedly on statements she had already made, in the hope of finding inconsistencies or contradictions and thus trap her into an admission that she had been lying. A typical session was that recorded in the dossier of the case for the 2nd July.

Crime at No. 8 Impasse Louvain   Dossier No. 0327

On July 2nd, We, Loubet, had brought before us the prisoner. Our examination of her was as follows:

Question: Today we propose to question you on your statements about the events on the night when your husband and your mother were murdered. I must make it clear at the outset that few people are prepared to believe the bizarre story which you have told the police.

Hassler: They may believe it or not as they choose, but what I have said is true.

Question: Let us first look at your story as a whole. You are saying that three people, strangely dressed, broke into your house to steal valuable documents that were in your possession as well as any money or jewels that they might find?

Hassler: That is correct.

Question: And you say they killed your husband and your mother who disturbed them in this robbery?

Hassler: It can only have happened like that, although of course I did not actually see them do it.

Question: And you expect me to believe that the only reason why they did not kill you as well was that they thought you were your daughter?

Hassler: Yes.

Question: I put it to you, it is inconceivable that anyone could possibly mistake you, a woman of over 40, for a young girl of seventeen.

Hassler: Why not? I was sleeping in my daughter's bed and the room was dark.

Question: Dark? Have you not already told us that the intruders were carrying lanterns?

Hassler: Yes.

Question: And was the light from these lanterns not bright enough for you to see and distinguish their faces, the colour of their hair and beards, the clothes they wore?

Hassler: Yes.

Question: But even so, not bright enough for the intruders to see that you were a middle-aged woman and not a girl?

Hassler: I repeat, it was clear that they mistook me for my daughter.

Question: Let us assume for the moment that what you say is true, however unlikely it seems. Here we have three cunning robbers who, because they were disturbed, killed two people in cold blood. Was it not folly for them to leave you, who might have been able to identify them, alive?

Hassler: As I said, the light was dim and they were disguised. They might well have considered that I would not be able to make out their faces and thus identify them.

Question: Now you are saying that the light was dim, although you were able to give the police a full and precise description of these people.

Hassler: The light was bright enough for me to see them.

Question: What's this? Have you forgotten that when you were proved mistaken in your identification of the American York, you gave as an excuse the poor light in the bedroom?

Hassler: I admit I was wrong about that and it was because I acted too hastily. Everyone was putting ideas into my head and it was they who suggested that this American must have been one of the men who broke into the house. I was overwrought and exhausted by the ordeal I had suffered and I convinced myself that I could recognize the American and that he must have been guilty.

95

Question: Let us examine another point. You told the police that it was around midnight when you were left bound to your bed. More than six hours must have passed before you called for help. Why was that?

Hassler: I was gagged.

Question: Are you saying it took you all those hours to spit the gag out of your mouth?

Hassler: As I have already said, when I was attacked and bound I fainted. It was only when I came out of my faint in the morning that I began trying to rid myself of the gag.

Question: You cannot expect us to believe that you were in a faint for more than six hours. Doctors will tell you that is impossible and that a fainting fit can only last for a few seconds, minutes at the most.

Hassler: In that case, I must have slept.

Question: Slept? Although you had been attacked, threatened with death, bound and gagged, you slept peacefully half the night?

Hassler: I can't help it. That's what happened.

Question: We must also look at the question of the bonds. The rope around your husband's neck was only loosely knotted and experts say the rope cannot have caused his death. And take your case. You have said that you dared not move or cry out or the rope would have strangled you, but both Monsieur Gide and your servant have said that the ropes which bound you were also not tied at all tightly, either at your wrists and ankles or around your neck.

Hassler: I can only tell you what I know to be true.

Question: We have evidence that the ropes which were used to bind you as well as those around your husband's throat were cut from a length of cord that was kept in your kitchen and the cottonwool for the gags came from a supply in your boudoir which you had bought to stuff cushions.

Hassler: If the police say so then it must be true, I suppose.

Question: Do you expect us to believe that a group of people who had planned to rob a house would leave it to chance that they could find ropes and gags there ready for them to use? Would·they not rather have brought these things with them?

Hassler: I believe that they expected to find the house empty or at the most occupied by my manservant. They may have known that I and my family had planned to spend the week-end in the country.

Question: In that case, why did they bother to come to your house disguised?

Hassler: How should I know? How should I understand the working of criminal minds? As you must have realized, Monsieur, I was brought up in a home where Christian virtues were placed first of all, where honesty was regarded just as highly as culture and social graces.

As he read through this and the other reports of the examination, Gautier felt a growing sense of disquiet. Although the examination of Josephine Hassler was prolonged, the magistrate Loubet was being neither as searching nor as inquisitorial in his questions as one would have expected in a murder case. Long hours were spent in cross-examining the prisoner on relatively unimportant issues and when she gave an unsatisfactory or evasive answer, Loubet seldom pursued the matter with more aggressive questions. As an example there was the time when he was questioning her about the rings which she had reported as having been stolen. Even though Courtrand had proved that she had been lying about the rings, when Loubet raised the matter the only explanation she gave him was more or less the same as the story she had told before. Instead of pressing the matter further and demanding from her the name of the wealthy admirer who was supposed to have given her the jewels and the name of the jeweller who had made the set of duplicate rings, Loubet merely listened to her reply and had then switched to a completely different tack.

In the meantime dozens of other witnesses were being questioned. Most of them could have had no possible connection with the crime nor any knowledge of it, but were only asked to testify on Josephine Hassler's character. A wide selection of such people was produced: nursemaids and servants who had known her as a child; neighbours from Beaucourt; ladies in Paris society who had met her only a few times and on purely social occasions. All Loubet's energies appeared to be directed towards blackening the prisoner's character and proving that she was capable of murdering her husband and her mother.

At times he also seemed to be trying, rather clumsily, to liven the interrogation with a touch of drama. There was the day when in reply to a question about discrepancies in her various statements, Josephine Hassler gave what was becoming her stock answer: that she had been so overwrought after the discovery of the murders that she had not known what she was saying.

On this occasion she added: 'All I could think of was that I had lost my mother.'

'So!' Loubet put in quickly. 'You were not concerned that you had also lost your husband?'

'Of course I was!'

'Come Madame, why not admit that you never loved your husband. You wanted him out of the way, so you could continue with your adulterous life without hindrance. That was why you killed him. That is why you strangled him with your bare hands.'

Josephine Hassler looked at him calmly and then held up her hands which, even after weeks in prison were soft and delicate and small. 'With these?' she asked Loubet quietly.

Throughout the long and arduous sessions of examination and despite these occasional brushes with the magistrate, Josephine Hassler remained self-possessed and she took every opportunity to complain about the rigours of prison life and about the ordeal to which she was being subjected. Gautier wondered whether her sang-froid sprang from a confidence in her own innocence or a secret knowledge of the eventual knowledge of the judicial examination.

One day when he was escorting her back to St Lazare from the Palais de Justice, she said to him without warning: 'You believe I'll be sent for trial, don't you, Inspector? You think that I'll be found guilty, sent to prison, perhaps to the guillotine.'

'No, Madame,' Gautier replied.

'Ah! So you have begun to believe me at last! You have decided I'm innocent.'

'That isn't what I said. I just happen to believe that whatever part you may have played in this crime, you won't be found guilty.'

XV

TOWARDS THE END of July, the examination of Josephine Hassler was finally concluded. The dossier of the case, which by this time ran into several thousand pages, was sent to the department of the Ministry of Justice known as the 'Chambre des Mises en Accusations', where five judges would study it and decide whether the accused should be sent on trial or released. The decision would not be announced for several days and the magistrate, Loubet, transferred his attention to another case. So Gautier found himself freed of the tedium of attending Josephine Hassler's examination each day and of having to carry out the magistrate's often tiresome instructions.

As Courtrand was attending an international conference of police chiefs in Geneva and since, so long as he was in theory working on the Impasse Louvain murders Gautier would not be assigned to another case, he found himself suddenly with the luxury of time to spare. The sensible course would have been to forget Impasse Louvain, put in a modest but energetic stint on paperwork at headquarters each day and use the rest of his time to catch up on his social and domestic life. But for some reason he found that he could not put the case out of his mind. A nagging belief that justice was being manipulated to serve political ends irritated him and moreover his ingrained stubbornness prevented him from taking the easy way out and abandoning the case to the lawyers.

He had two ideas, neither of them positive enough to be called a lead, which he wished to follow. One day he arranged to meet Surat at his office early in the morning and gave him his instructions.

'You'll find the address of that American artist, York, in the police dossier of the case. A girl named Mimi lives in the same building as him, a small-time model and part-time prostitute. Not long ago she was badly beaten up at some place in the Rue des Moulins. I want to know all about the assault, including the name of the man who did it. After you've seen the girl, go to the Ritz. You'll be on more difficult ground there because the hotel won't want to give information about the guests, but try to screw it out of the management. I want to know how many times this Colonel de Clermont has stayed in the hotel over the past two years, the length of his visits and anything else you can find out about the man: his habits, his friends, whether he throws his money about and if so on what.'

Leaving the Sûreté, Gautier took an omnibus to the Gare de l'Est and caught a train bound for Montbéliard. It was a slow train which dawdled lazily through the countryside, stopping at a succession of small towns, the names of some of which he had never even heard before. He left it at Toussaint, the last stop before Montbéliard and an overgrown village which had pretensions to being a market town. A man driving a horse and trap was waiting for him at the station, for the local police had been alerted to his visit by telephone the previous day.

Before setting out for the Château d'Ivry, he called in to see the police who confirmed what he had been told over the telephone, namely that Colonel de Clermont was in residence at the château. He did not explain the purpose of his visit, nor make any mention of the Impasse Louvain case, but he did encourage a little exchange of gossip about the local landowner. What he heard bore out the report that Surat had made. Colonel Gerard de Clermont was not popular in the neighbourhood. He neither made social advances to others nor welcomed them himself, he was close with his money and never gave donations to charity nor provided gifts at baptisms, birthdays or weddings. On the other hand he paid his bills promptly, went to church on Sundays and had not, as many other well-to-do landowners, flooded the district with a string of bastards by local girls.

Armed with this unpromising information, Gautier was driven from the police station to the château, which proved to be a large, ugly house of grey stone set in flat parkland about five kilometres from Toussaint. His ring at the front door was answered by a manservant to whom he gave his official card, explaining that he wished to see Colonel de Clermont. The man disappeared with the card and returned shortly.

'The master says he does not receive visits from police inspectors and that if you wish to speak to the staff, you should use the servants' entrance.'

'Does he now?' Gautier asked roughly.

Taking the card back, he wrote on the reverse side of it: 'I have come here in connection with the recent arrest of Madame Josephine Hassler. If you prefer me to discuss the matter with your servants I shall of course be glad to do so.'

Placing the card in an envelope which he sealed, he gave it back to the colonel's servant and told him: 'Take that to your master.'

A few minutes later he was admitted to the house. The entrance hall was bleak and cheerless, made even more unwelcoming by the heads of animals, trophies of the chase, which stared down from the walls, their eyes fixed in the bright stare of death. Following the manservant, Gautier passed a half-open door and saw standing in the drawing-room beyond a woman, who was perhaps 25 and looked ten years older. She watched him pass with anxious, faded eyes.

He was shown into a study which overlooked a terrace at the back of the house and in which a man sat writing at a large desk. Colonel Gerard de Clermont was tall and lean and dark. He was also athletic and strong and looked as though he might be proud of his strength; the kind of man who might vault a five-barred gate or just as easily throw an apple up into the air and slice it in two with a sword. He looked up at Gautier.

'You policemen are getting above yourselves. How dare you presume to call on me without an appointment?'

'The law does not concern itself with social niceties,' Gautier replied.

'Keep up that attitude and you won't be an inspector much longer.'

'And you, Colonel, are no longer a soldier. You command no one; certainly not me.'

Although he had not been invited to sit down, Gautier drew a chair up to the desk and sat down facing de Clermont. He did not have a very high regard for army officers, for the servile respect which they paid to those of higher rank than themselves, for their arrogance towards those whom they believed to be their inferiors. In his experience, no matter how brave they might have been in the field, army officers lacked moral courage and backed down in confrontations.

'I'm investigating the recent murders at Impasse Louvain in Paris, Colonel,' he said calmly.

'So you wrote on your card.' Gautier's card lay on the desk and de Clermont thumped it with his fist angrily. 'And how the devil is that supposed to concern me? Tell me that!'

'In no way, Colonel. But I have instructions from the examining magistrate to find people who knew Madame Hassler and who would be able to testify as to her character.'

'Well, that does not include me.'

'But you know the lady?'

'She was born not far from here. I know her family slightly.'

'Perhaps I should tell you, Colonel, we know that a few days before her arrest Madame Hassler lunched with you in a private apartment in the Ritz Hotel.'

Alarm flared briefly in de Clermont's eyes to be replaced almost at once by a look of uncontrollable fury. He shouted at Gautier: 'Are you saying that you've had the impertinence to spy on me?'

'Colonel, until that day we were not even aware of your existence. Madame Hassler was under surveillance as part of routine police procedure in a murder case.'

'And now you've jumped to the conclusion that I must somehow be involved in this crime.'

'Not at all. We have come to see you simply because you know Madame Hassler.' Gautier paused to add effect to his next remark. 'And you must know her well since she came unchaperoned to lunch with you in a hotel suite.'

The comment did not needle de Clermont as much as Gautier had expected. He rose from his desk and crossed to the window, where he stood looking out over the terrace and the fields beyond. Gautier noticed a deep scar slanting across his left cheek which was partly concealed by his moustaches and sideboards. The scar and his short-cropped, black hair coupled with the deep-set eyes and hawkish nose, gave him the look of an assassin.

'These murders have caused me some embarrassment, Inspector,' he said finally and there could be no mistaking the change in his attitude.

'Why is that, Colonel?'

'I have to admit that I have been friendly with the lady. But then, as you must have discovered by now, so have a good many other men.'

'If she were to be put on trial, would you be ready to give evidence about her character?'

'Good God, Inspector, surely in view of my er—relationship with the lady, I could not be expected to speak about her character!' De Clermont laughed; the confidential laugh of one man to another about a woman of their acquaintance, a masculine laugh loaded with innuendo. 'After all, man, why me? Why not a minister or some other public figure? Why not the late president? He did die for love of her!'

The colonel laughed again and looked at Gautier. They were to be friends now, Gautier supposed and that must mean he was to be promoted to temporary colonel. He said: 'There is one question which I am expected to ask you, Colonel. Were you at the Hasslers' house at any time on the day of the murders?'

'Good God, no! I would have been the first to come forward and tell the police if I had. In the army we are taught to recognize our public duty.'

'One final point. Did you ever give Madame Hassler any gifts of jewelry?'

'Certainly not!'

'No rings? No pearls?'

De Clermont's face took on an expression of sullen displeasure. 'If you're referring to that wretched necklace which she was always talking about, then it's supposed to be worth almost more than my château.'

'Did she never mention who gave it to her?'

'Not by name, but by all the hints she dropped it could only have been the late president.'

Moving away from the window, de Clermont pulled on a bell

cord. The act was enough to create a diversion and interrupt their conversation. Before it could be re-started, he turned to Gautier and smiled a fellow officer's smile.

'If you've finished cross-examining me, Inspector, let me persuade you to take a glass of something. It's just about aperitif time.'

Gautier recognized the gesture as one of lordly dismissal. He was prepared to accept it because he judged there was nothing more he could get out of de Clermont for the time being and taking a drink with the man might at least keep the door open. The manservant appeared in answer to the bell with a decanter of port and two matching glasses on a silver tray.

As they sipped their drinks, he noticed the colonel glance at him more than once; thoughtful, appraising glances. Eventually de Clermont said: 'How is Madame Hassler standing up to the juge d'instruction? They tell me these fellows can be pretty ruthless in the questions they ask.'

'I think one might say that she's holding her own.'

'Good, good!' He glanced at Gautier again. 'You've been present at the interrogations, have you?'

'Yes. Most of the time.'

'What sort of questions has he been asking her?'

'Very wide ranging. That's how the system works.'

De Clermont hesitated briefly and then asked: 'Has Madame Hassler mentioned my name by any chance?'

'No.'

'Well, I warn you she might.' The colonel laughed without amusement. 'You know what women are like. More than once Josephine has asked me if I loved her and whether I'd like to marry her. Of course I pointed out that she was already married.'

'But you were not interested in marriage anyway?'

'Heavens, no! But one doesn't like to hurt a girl's feelings and I suppose she may just possibly have jumped to the conclusion that I'd rather fancy marrying her.'

'And now, of course, she's free to marry.'

'Precisely. Slightly awkward for me, I can tell you.'

'Well, so far she hasn't even spoken about you, either to me or to the juge d'instruction.'

'I'm delighted to hear it.'

The colonel finished his port in a swift gulp. Now that he had learnt what he wished to know, he clearly wanted to rid himself of Gautier as quickly as possible. Putting his glass down he said: 'Very glad to have had this little chat, Inspector. It clears the air. We must keep in touch. Can you find your own way out, do you think?'

On his way out through the hall, Gautier smiled to himself at the contrast between de Clermont's manner at his arrival and at his departure. The colonel seemed to have convinced himself that Gautier had come all the way from Paris to reassure him. The door to the drawing-room was still open when he passed it and the same woman was standing beyond it. She looked at him and her lips twitched in what might have been intended as a smile.

When he reached Paris it was evening but, feeling that his long day had been frustratingly unproductive, he went to Sûreté headquarters in the hope that Surat might have left some account of his own day's investigations on Gautier's desk. He was not disappointed and found a report waiting for him in a sealed envelope marked for his attention. It was written in the round, laboriously fashioned script which he could instantly recognize as his subordinate's handwriting.

CONFIDENTIAL REPORT

On your instructions I went to Rue Lépic in Montmartre to interview the woman Marie-France Despard, known professionally as 'Mimi'. She was totally unco-operative, denied that she had ever been associated with any brothel or other establishment in Rue des Moulins and professed complete ignorance of any assault or similar incident. She repeated these statements so vehemently, even when I threatened to bring her in for questioning, that I began to believe that a mistake might have been made. However after leaving her apartment I made enquiries among her neighbours who confirmed that she works in an establishment at number 3, Rue des Moulins. I then went to the Ritz Hotel where I was able to establish the dates on which Colonel Gerard de Clermont has stayed there during the last two years. These are given on the attached sheet. It would appear that Colonel de Clermont has been in the habit of coming to Paris about every three months or so for several years. Recently his visits have been much more frequent. As you will see he spent the night of 31 May, which as you know was the date of the Impasse Louvain murders, in Paris. Thinking that you might be interested in his movements on that night, I made further enquiries among the hotel staff and learned that the colonel came to Paris on that particular occasion to attend a banquet at his club, the Cercle Agricole. The doorman at the Ritz remembers him leaving the hotel early in the evening and returning at about eleven o'clock. Subsequently I went to the Cercle Agricole to check with the secretariat of the club who were able to confirm that the colonel had attended the banquet.

signed: F. Surat.

Gautier glanced through the list of dates attached to the report. They showed, as Surat had stated, that over the last few months de Clermont had been coming to Paris twice and sometimes three times a month. That might suggest a growing infatuation for Josephine Hassler. On the other hand, as the colonel himself had remarked, he was only one of several men who had been enjoying her favours and there was not the slightest evidence to show that he had in any way been connected with the murders at Impasse Louvain.

Still dissatisfied with the day's achievements, Gautier locked Surat's report in his desk, left Sûreté headquarters and, remembering that he had eaten nothing all day, crossed the Seine to a small restaurant near the Halles. There he was served with a huge dish of cassoulet, a hunk of fresh bread and a carafe of red wine. Then he walked up to Rue des Moulins.

Number 3 was well known to the Paris police, although they seldom paid it any of the routine precautionary visits which they made to the many other brothels of the city. Popularly known as La Maison des Anglais, number 3 was frequented by men of society, members of the Jockey Club, visiting American millionaires, the diplomatic corps and royalty. Before he became King of England, the Prince of Wales, it was rumoured, had been a regular visitor during his frequent trips to Paris and this was the origin of its nickname. People said he used to fill a special silver bath with vintage Champagne for the ablutions of the girl who was his choice for the evening. As good Frenchmen, the police understood very well that it would be indiscreet and possibly embarrassing if they were to drop in on a 'maison close' with such a clientèle.

Outside the house there was nothing to show the kind of pleasures it offered, not even the large illuminated street number which was the accepted sign of a brothel. Inside the front door a liveried servant took Gautier's hat and showed him into a large room, which by the elegance of its furnishings might easily have been a drawing-room in Avenue du Bois. Three men in evening dress were playing cards at a table opposite the door, while two girls in stylish dresses were re-charging the brandy glasses at their elbows. In another corner a handsome, silver-haired man whom Gautier recognized as a duke and a former member of the Senate, was sitting on a Louis XIV sofa next to a beautiful Japanese girl.

A woman of about 50, expensively dressed, came forward, arms outstretched, towards Gautier. 'My friend!' she exclaimed. 'How lovely to see you again! Come and tell me your news.' She called out to the footman who was still standing by the door: 'Feliçien, fetch some Champagne for Monsieur.'

Gautier knew he had never seen the woman before and he began: 'Don't think me impolite, Madame, but—'

'Let's sit over there,' the woman said, interrupting his protest and pointing towards two chairs at the end of the room farthest from the card players.

Suddenly realizing what the woman was trying to do, Gautier followed her to the chairs, sat down and waited until the Champagne was brought and poured out for them. Then he asked her: 'How did you know I was from the police, Madame?'

'One learns to sense it, Monsieur. And it is very obliging of you to play my little game so my guests will not know.'

'I haven't come to cause you any trouble but merely to talk to one of your girls.'

'Which one?'

'Marie-France Despard. I understand that she calls herself "Mimi" professionally.'

'Is she in trouble? Perhaps there's something I could do.'

'No, Madame, I think not. I just want to ask her a few questions.'

'That can easily be arranged. Would you mind very much seeing her in one of our rooms upstairs?'

'Whatever causes you least inconvenience.'

'If you would wait a moment then.'

The woman left the room. While she was away, Gautier looked around him as he sipped his Champagne. Even to his inexpert eye it was obvious that the cut-glass chandeliers in the room, the heavy gilt-framed mirrors and the paintings were all genuine and expensive. All the men to be seen were wearing evening dress. He had heard that the bedrooms were also lavishly decorated, each in a different style – Spanish, Venetian, Moorish, Scandinavian – to suit the mood or the inclinations of the clients. He could see no sign of impropriety, no scantily-clad girls, no drunkenness, no bawdy language. The rich, he concluded, evidently took their pleasures like gentlemen.

Presently the woman who had received him returned and said: 'Go up to the first floor. The young lady is waiting in the English room; that is the third room on the right.'

Following her instructions, he mounted an imposing staircase and made his way along a corridor on the first floor to the third door on the right. It opened on to a room that was in semi-darkness, the only light coming from an oil lamp which threw grotesque shadows on the ceiling. The walls were a plain, stark white, studded with hooks and nails from which hung a selection of chains and whips and manacles. In one corner stood a life-size figure carved in wood of a Christian martyr, St Sebastian perhaps, whose body, bound to a stake, was pierced by arrows.

When his eyes grew accustomed to the gloom, Gautier saw that a girl was lying on a wooden bed in the centre of the room. She wore a long shift of a white diaphanous material and little more and her dark hair hung loose to her shoulders. At the head and foot of the bed were leather straps by which a prostrate victim could be secured before flagellation. The room, one supposed, was the torture chamber of which he had heard speak, provided for English visitors since the English were reputed to enjoy the particular perversion which it offered. Realizing that the woman who ran the establishment must have deliberately chosen this room as the most appropriate for a policeman to interrogate one of her girls, Gautier was amused by her sense of humour.

He said to the girl on the bed: 'Are you Marie-France Despard?'

'Yes, I am.'

'Then you can sit up. I'm from the Sûreté.

She sat up quickly and he noticed that she wore slave bangles on her wrists and ankles, intended no doubt to heighten the atmosphere of primitive savagery. 'What do you want?'

'The answers to certain questions; answers which you refused to give my colleague this morning.'

'I can only tell you, as I told him, that I know nothing.'

'Come now, Mimi, you lied to him when you said you didn't work here. Isn't that so?'

'Well, I know nothing of the other affair, the supposed assault.'

Gautier sighed and shook his head. 'In that case I shall have no alternative but to take you to the nearest police post where we can discover whether your registration as a prostitute is in order. And that, Mimi, will be the end of your job here, since Madame would never employ girls who are in trouble with the police.'

She called him a filthy name, using an adjective that was much in vogue among soldiers in North Africa but rarely used by young ladies in Paris. Then she said truculently: 'What do you want to know?'

'For a start the name of the man who beat you up.'

'Men who come to this place don't give their names. And anyway it was his first visit here, so I didn't know him. He told me to call him Nicki.'

'A name he had invented, no doubt. Describe him.'

'He was not tall but very broad and powerful; going bald, with a thick moustache and a short, neatly-trimmed beard. Twenty years ago, before he started going to fat, he must have been quite a man. He wasn't French of course.'

'English?'

'His accent could have been English but his manners were too coarse and brutal. The Englishmen we get here are always beautifully behaved.'

'Even when they whip you? That's nice to know. Anything else?'

Mimi thought for a while before replying. 'I would say he was a man who was used to getting what he wanted, women included, without ever paying. He couldn't have been in an establishment like this very often before.'

'What makes you say that?'

'That was the start of the row we had, that and the drink. He kept repeating that back home he didn't have to pay for women; they were only too glad to sleep with him. Finally I grew sick of it and told him I'd want double to make love with anyone so fat and vulgar. He slapped me across the face so I took off my shoe and hit him with it. That was a mistake. He went quite crazy, turned as red as a beetroot, swore and punched me. Trying to get away from him I fell and hurt my ribs, but that didn't stop him and he grabbed my throat as though he meant to kill me. He might easily have done so, but then this other man rushed into the room just in time and dragged Nicki off.'

'What man was that?'

'A burly fellow, soberly dressed, who had arrived with the group and was sitting down in the hall all the time sipping beer.'

'A bodyguard, perhaps.'

'Perhaps. They say he goes everywhere with this Nicki.' She made a contemptuous noise and put one hand up to her throat. 'Not that he'd ever neéd a bodyguard. A warder would be better; to stop him going right off his head and killing somebody. It couldn't have been a servant, for he was carrying a pile of money. It was him who called up Madame and settled for the damage.'

'The damage to your feelings, I suppose.' Gautier pointed at the instruments of torture which ringed the room around them. 'Perhaps it was all this which sparked off his violence. If you encourage sadism you should expect to get hurt once in a while.'

'We weren't even in here. We were in the Byzantine room.'

'Why didn't you lodge a complaint of assault with the police?'

'For the same reason as I'm telling you all this: I didn't want to lose my job. And the compensation they paid me was generous, I'll give him that. So why should I drag in the police?'

'Why indeed? Would you know where I might be likely to find this Nicki?'

'No, unless you try Maxim's. He told me he dines there almost every night.'

Leaving La Maison des Anglais, Gautier decided that exercise might stimulate his brain and he walked home. Although he did not have much for a day spent in following hunches, he was not discouraged. The juge d'instruction, Loubet, had accused Josephine Hassler of conspiring to have her husband murdered by paid assassins so she would be free to earn money by a life of coquetry. Newspapers had hinted that the killer was some scoundrel, a servant perhaps, whom she had taken to her bed and who might now be blackmailing her. Gautier did not believe either theory. He was looking for a man with money and social position because he was convinced that Josephine Hassler was too class-conscious and too fastidious to become involved in any sordid affair with sordid people. He also suspected that he should be looking for a man whom sexual passion or jealousy could drive into a homicidal frenzy.

The man who had attacked Mimi at La Maison des Anglais appeared to satisfy both descriptions. She had said that he was always accompanied by a retainer or bodyguard and Gautier remembered Claudine's description of the man who waited in the lane outside Josephine Hassler's house whenever she was entertaining a certain male friend. That could be just coincidence and a slender one at that, but Gautier was prepared to spend a little more time on it, to probe a little further.

When he reached home, Suzanne was already in bed but not yet asleep. She offered to get up and cook him a meal but he told her he had already eaten. As he undressed he felt a nagging sense of guilt that he had been leaving her alone too much, unnecessarily, because the enquiries he had been making could easily have waited until the following day. Not many women would have accepted the neglect and the loneliness without complaint.

As he lay next to her in bed, he found himself thinking of La Maison des Anglais, of the almost naked body of Mimi, of her large, provocative mouth. The memory invoked a stab of desire and this, coupled with affection and remorse, triggered a sudden impulse. Reaching out he placed his fingers just below Suzanne's breast and began very gently to stroke her in a way which invariably aroused her.

'Please, Jean-Paul, not tonight,' she said and pushed his hand away.

XVI

WHEN THE FIACRE drew to a halt in Rue Royale and he helped Claudine out, Gautier, in spite of the cynicism bred by his years in the police force, could not suppress a feeling of excitement. Maxim's was easily the most celebrated restaurant in Paris, virtually a club for gentlemen of society and a glittering shop-window for the most expensive, the most beautiful and the most coveted women of the demi-monde. Stories of the scandalous liaisons which were paraded there every night, of the restaurant's gaiety and extravagance, were breathlessly repeated and admired by the whole of Paris.

It was not so much the reputation of Maxim's, however, which filled Gautier with pleasurable anticipation, but a sense of the occasion. There he was, walking into a great restaurant, wearing as convention demanded, full evening dress and escorting a girl of exceptional loveliness. When he had called for Claudine at her apartment, the transformation in her appearance had astounded him. The untidy and impatient gamin charm had been replaced by poise, self-possession and a hint of hauteur. The long, full-skirted dress she was wearing could not be faulted for style or cut or colour, nor could the long white gloves and the corsage worn, as fashion dictated, at the neck.

Diffidently he had sent her the previous day a 'petit bleu' or message by the pneumatic telegraph, inviting her to dine with him in formal dress. Knowing her scorn for social conventions, he had been prepared for a refusal, but she had accepted without comment and apparently without surprise.

They went into Maxim's and the maître d'hotel showed them to a table opposite the stage where a gipsy orchestra was already playing. Only a short time previously Maxime Gaillard, the owner of the restaurant, had allowed it to be decorated in the daring style of 'art nouveau', a decision which had sparked off impassioned controversy, drawing extravagant praise from some, hostility and abuse from the art critics.

Flowers were the dominant motif throughout. The carved wooden screen, the tables and seats, the plaster mouldings of the cornices, the gilded frames of the enormous mirrors, were all shaped in pattern of flowers and trailing leaves in convoluted spirals. As if that were not enough, there were real flowers as well, everywhere, large clumps of azaleas and gladioli and irises in the corners of the room and on the staircase which led to the balcony. The chairs and wall seats were upholstered in red leather in startling contrast to the incredible whiteness of table cloths and napkins. The colours, the myriad lights of the crystal chandeliers reflected in the mirrors, the sparkle of silver on white tablecloths and, more than all this, the sheer opulence of the place dazzled Gautier.

When they were seated facing each other across the table with a bottle of Mumm Cordon Rouge in an ice-bucket beside them, Claudine suddenly laughed.

'What on earth are we doing here?' she demanded. 'A policeman and a second-rate artist's model. It's a surrealist fairy story!'

'Excellent! All fairy stories have happy endings.'

'Why did you bring me here and not your wife?'

'Unreasonable questions run the risk of unreasonable answers.'

'But why?'

'Men don't bring their wives to Maxim's.'

The urchin grin reappeared. 'Touché!'

As the evening passed the restaurant, only moderately full when they arrived, began to grow more crowded. Gautier recognized celebrities among the diners and pointed them out to Claudine. At one table, her regular table he had heard, Caroline Otero, the second or perhaps the third most sought-after cocotte in Paris, sat accompanied by three men. Nearby were the Prince de Selignac and a very rich banker named Krief, who were entertaining two ballet dancers from the Opera. The President of the Jockey Club, a man of almost 80 with fine sideboards and a monocle, was whispering persuasively to a handsome widow of perhaps 40, who had just opened a couturier's in Place Vendôme that was all the vogue among rich ladies.

'How did this place become so popular?' Claudine asked.

'A mixture of snobbism and fashion. The French will do anything, sacrifice anything, to conform with the fashion of the day.'

'Yes, but how did this fashion start?'

'By sheer chance. It was a very modest eating place until a few years ago and then one evening the great cocotte, Irma de Montigny, arrived at the much more exclusive Weber's at the other end of Rue Royale to find that a careless waiter had given away her table. In a prima donna's rage she stamped out with her entourage, came here, liked it and never went back to Weber's. Almost overnight Maxim's became the place in Paris for the demi-monde.'

While they were eating – 'Sole Nantua, Noisette de Chevreuil à Bayonne and Bombe Alhambra – Gautier kept looking round the room, wondering if he might see anyone who matched the description Mimi had given him of the man who had beaten her up at La Maison des Anglais. Late in the evening, when they had almost finished their meal, a noisy party arrived; two girls accompanied by four men who, Gautier decided, could only be Russian. One wore the uniform of a Russian army colonel while the other three spoke a heavily accented French which they punctuated from time to time with strange, guttural oaths. The man who seemed to be host to the party was massively broad, balding and had moustaches and a beard which matched Mimi's description.

When next a waiter came to their table, Gautier asked him: 'Who are those foreign gentlemen over there? The one in the splendid uniform and his party?'

'They are Russian, Monsieur. The short, bald gentleman is the new Russian ambassador.'

'I see. Does he come here often?'

'He has only been in Paris for a few months but already he's one of our most regular customers. He and his friends come almost every night. And the money they spend! One evening they played some game with gold coins which they kept rolling across the floor. Next morning the cleaners found no less than fourteen coins, lying in the corners and under the seats, which the gentlemen had left behind. Worth hundreds of francs, they were.'

Gautier felt a quickening anticipation, quite different to the sensation he had experienced as he had led Claudine into the restaurant. For almost the first time since he had been called to the Hasslers' house on the Sunday morning after the murders, he sensed that he was about to lift at least a corner of the carpet under which the truth lay hidden.

'So this is not just a social occasion!' Claudine remarked after the waiter had left. 'I should have known.'

'I didn't think you'd mind if I combined a little business with what for me is the very great pleasure of your company.' She made a rude noise expressing disbelief at the flattery and reinforced it with an even ruder word. Gautier went on: 'Besides it was the only way I could afford to bring you here.'

'I'll accept that. What case are you working on, anyway?'

'Still the same one.'

'Hassler's murder? I thought his old bitch of a wife had been arrested.'

'She has and she's to be sent for trial. That was announced only today.'

'But you don't believe she's guilty?'

'Guilty or not, someone else must have been involved; for Josephine Hassler couldn't possibly have murdered two people unaided.'

They finished their dinner with two glasses of Grand Marnier. When Gautier called for a cigar, Claudine demanded and smoked a cigarette. Anywhere else but in Maxim's this might have caused a minor sensation because for women to smoke in public was still unacceptable, but Maxim's was accustomed to eccentricity. Seeing her parade her contempt for convention gave Gautier an idea.

'You could earn your dinner by helping me in a small way,' he suggested.

'How?'

'Do you see that short, bald man in the noisy gang just behind me? Give him a few encouraging glances. Nothing too obvious or vulgar, you understand.'

'So that's how you hope to pay for this extravagant dinner! Haven't you heard that pimping is against the law?'

'Just a few sexy looks. It won't go any further than that. I just want to see how he reacts.'

'I'm not very good at that sort of thing, but I'll try.'

Gautier was sitting with his back towards the Russian party and while he could see the sidelong glances and faint smiles which from time to time Claudine threw in their direction, he had no means of judging whether they were having the desired effect on the bald man. After about ten minutes, however, a waiter appeared and under the pretext of sweeping crumbs from the tablecloth, he slipped a folded piece of paper to Claudine which Gautier was not supposed to notice.

She unfolded it and read it quietly: 'Mademoiselle, if you wish to free yourself of your present company I will put my coach at your disposal. The coachman will take you to a place where you and I can meet later. If you will do me the honour of accepting this invitation, just nod your head.'

Taking the note from her fingers, Gautier jumped up and crossed the restaurant to the table where the Russians were sitting. He looked at the bald man, held up the note and demanded insolently: 'Was it you, Sir, who had the impudence and ill-manners to send this to the young lady at my table?'

The bald man looked at him, clearly disconcerted by this unexpected confrontation. 'I beg your pardon, Monsieur?'

The Russian colonel said angrily: 'Are you aware, Monsieur, that you are speaking to His Excellency, the Grand Duke Varaslav?'

'Did you or did you not send this note?' Gautier demanded, ignoring the interruption.

'We in Russia,' the ambassador said coldly, retreating into a defensive hauteur, 'do not speak with strangers, especially on the subject of women.'

'Evidently. Perhaps if you had spoken a little more freely Madame Josephine Hassler would not now be standing trial for murder.'

The effect of this sneer on the Russian was devastating. His face, already flushed with an excess of good living, turned slowly crimson. Panic, like a danger signal, lit up his eyes then died away to be replaced, first by fear and then by anger. Jumping to his feet he lashed out with the back of his hand and caught Gautier a stinging blow across the cheek.

'My seconds will call on you, Monsieur.'

Gautier bowed slightly, said nothing, but took one of his business cards from his pocket and placed it on the table in front of the grand duke. The colonel quickly snatched it up to read it.

'Ambassadors do not duel with policemen, your excellency,' he told the grand duke and then turning to Gautier added: 'In Russia we do not even speak to them.'

'No, you take the coward's way, just as now you allow Josephine Hassler to stand trial alone.'

To Gautier's disappointment, this calculated gibe did not sting the ambassador into a further revealing outburst. Instead the Russian remained silent, although he was clearly having the greatest difficulty in suppressing his anger.

Leaving them Gautier walked back to his own table, aware that most of the diners in the restaurant were staring at him. In spite of the raised voices and the resounding slap, however, the incident provoked no more than a mild interest. Maxim's had known far more tempestuous quarrels and even though duelling was supposed to be illegal, the sight of a challenge was still in no way unusual.

As he crossed the room, Gautier noticed a man with heavy drooping moustaches and a brown bowler hat peering into the restaurant from the vestibule.

'Now at last I know what it feels like to have men fight over me,' Claudine mocked him when he reached her.

'No fight, I'm afraid.'

'A pity! But did that little piece of contrived melodrama tell you what you came here to find out?'

'I'm not certain yet.'

Soon afterwards they left Maxim's. Outside in Rue Royale coachmen waiting for their masters were gossiping with two uniformed chauffeurs of motor cars. The man in the brown bowler hat was with them and for an instant Gautier saw his face clearly in the light from one of the gilded lanterns over the entrance to the restaurant.

'That man!' Claudine exclaimed suddenly pointing towards him.

'He's the one whom Félix Hassler and I saw standing outside his house. Remember, I told you about him.'

'Are you sure?'

'Absolutely certain.'

'I know him too.'

Gautier had recognized the man in the bowler as Fénèlon, a former police inspector, now retired, under whom he had once served for a time in the fifteenth arrondissement. He led Claudine towards him.

'Inspector Fénèlon?'

Fénèlon did not seem surprised to see him. 'Yes. Let me see, you're Gautier aren't you?'

'That's right. Also an inspector now, in Sûreté headquarters.'

'Well, well.' Fénèlon looked at Gautier's evening clothes and then at Claudine. 'The pay must be better than in my day.'

'What are you doing these days?'

'Got my own business. A detective agency. Quite a nice little proposition now that divorce is becoming so fashionable.'

'Are you here on a job?'

Fénèlon nodded and winked. 'That's right. And a good, steady job too.' He pulled a business card out of his pocket. 'Drop in and see me at my office sometime. I'll tell you all about it and we can have a chat about the old days.'

'I might do just that.'

The fiacre which the doorman at Maxim's had fetched for them was waiting. Gautier nodded to Fénèlon, helped Claudine in and they were driven off in the direction of Montmartre. When they reached the vicinity of the Butte, the driver insisted on dropping them off in Boulevard Rochechouart, saying that his horse was too tired to climb up the hill to where Claudine lived. He was obviously not pleased, having assumed that a client from Maxim's would have been heading not for the grimy suburbs but for a more fashionable district. There was little likelihood of his picking up a return fare to the centre of Paris from Montmartre. Drivers of fiacres were an independent, often truculent breed and Gautier decided not to risk spoiling the evening by exercising his police authority.

So he and Claudine climbed the long flight of stone steps that led to Place Ravignan and walked from there to her apartment. When they stopped outside her door and he held out his hand to say goodnight, she asked: 'Aren't you coming in?'

'Isn't it rather late to sit for my portrait?'

'Yes.'

'And really I don't think I want any more to drink.' Privately Gautier was thinking that she might not have much drink to offer and certainly none to spare.

Raising one hand she ran her finger along the length of his jaw, the same gesture that she had used after the first evening they had spent together. She said seriously: 'That isn't what I was offering you.'

XVII

THE JUGE D'INSTRUCTION, Loubet, had an office in the Palais
de Justice next to the room in which he had been conducting the
examination of Josephine Hassler. He was a small, slightly paunchy
man with moustaches and beard trimmed in the style still popular
among middle-aged and elderly Parisians who liked to model
themselves on the King of England. This admiration for Edward
was part of the love-hate emotion which French society felt for
England. Politically Britain was still bitterly resented and memories
of Fashoda still rankled; so much so that for years Queen Victoria
had been the subject of abusive and sometimes scurrilous cartoons
in French newspapers. Yet the manners and dress of the British
were assiduously imitated. Every home of any standing had an
English governess for the children whom it dressed in sailor suits,
while men hunted foxes, started gentlemen's clubs and sent their
evening shirts to be laundered and starched in London.

'Well, Inspector, you asked to see me,' Loubet said to Gautier.
'What is it about?'

'The Impasse Louvain affair, Sir.'

'But the examination of the woman has been concluded. The
dossier has been passed to the Chambre des Mises en Accusation
and so my part in the process is finished.'

'Even so, I thought you should know that I believe I may have
discovered Madame Hassler's accomplice in the murders.'

'And who is that?'

'The Russian ambassador in Paris.'

Loubet looked at him thoughtfully. 'In that case, Inspector, you
had better sit down and tell me about it.'

Briefly Gautier told him of the Grand Duke Varaslav's behaviour at La Maison des Anglais and of why he believed that the

man whom the manservant Mansard had seen outside the Hasslers' house on the night of the murder must have been the private detective Fénèlon. He did not say anything about his own confrontation with the grand duke at Maxim's.

When he had finished Loubet remarked: 'Your evidence is scarcely conclusive, Inspector.'

'I realize that, but a few enquiries might easily produce definite proof.'

'And so you are asking me for my authority to make such enquiries?'

'Yes, Sir.'

Loubet leant back in his chair and stroked his beard thoughtfully. During the examination of Josephine Hassler, Gautier had formed the impression that the judge was conscientious, intelligent and scrupulously fair, a man who had accepted his post not for love of power or personal ambition, but because he respected and valued the law. That was why he had come to consult Loubet instead of approaching one of the senior officials at the Sûreté.

'Your first step, Inspector, would be to question this detective person, I suppose?'

'Yes, Sir.'

'There can be no harm in that but until you have much stronger evidence that the grand duke was actually at Impasse Louvain on the night of the murders, you should make no attempt to question either him or any of the embassy staff.'

'Those conditions will make my investigations very difficult.'

'I'm afraid so, but remember that diplomats have certain privileges and of course you have no right to enter the embassy of a foreign power uninvited.'

'Diplomatic status wouldn't protect anyone involved in murder, though?'

'There are other considerations to be taken into account. Remember, Gautier, that our government is anxious to preserve good relations with Russia,' Loubet said and then smiled as he added: 'But then I'm sure we can rely on you to be tactful and discreet. The prefect has a very high opinion of you.'

Before he left Gautier decided to ask the judge one last question.

'Am I right in thinking, Sir, that you did not appear surprised when I mentioned the grand duke's name?'

Loubet sighed. 'Between you and me, his excellency has been causing certain problems, Gautier. I'm not suggesting for a moment that he could possibly be a murderer – that is inconceivable – but, well, there has been trouble with women, particularly with women of a certain class.'

As he left the Palais de Justice, Gautier found himself thinking about what Loubet had said. It did indeed seem inconceivable that the ambassador could possibly have been party to a deliberate murder. The man might have an overpowering urge for sex and was certainly promiscuous, but that made it less likely rather than more, that he would kill for a woman. There was no shortage of women in Paris to satisfy all his tastes. The manservant Mansard and Claudine might well both have been mistaken and the person seen in the lane outside the house might have been a passing stranger. Even the grand duke's behaviour at Maxim's could be explained. Had he been secretly involved with Josephine Hassler, he would be only too anxious to conceal the fact at a time when she had become the centre of a major scandal.

From the Palais de Justice he took an omnibus to the Place de la République and from there made his way to Rue Gassonville, which proved to be a narrow street leading off Rue Réaumur. The buildings in the street were shoddy and housed the offices of a large number of small businesses, attracted to the neighbourhood no doubt by a belief that the proximity of newspaper offices would lend them respectability.

Fénèlon's office was on the fourth floor, reached after a tramp up a staircase in almost total darkness. Obeying the instructions on the door, Gautier knocked and entered. Inside a youth of about eighteen wearing a black suit and paper cuffs to protect his shirt, was sitting with his boots on a desk reading a pornographic book.

When Gautier asked for Fénèlon, the youth said: 'He's not here.'

'When will he be here?'

'I can't say.' The youth had not bothered to take his feet off the desk and was not at all pleased at having his reading interrupted.

'Look, son,' Gautier said, deciding that a small measure of

authority might save his time, 'I'm from the Sûreté. Inspector Gautier. Either you give me some answers and a little civility or I'll take you down to headquarters.'

The youth jumped up in alarm. 'I'm sorry, Monsieur l'Inspecteur, but honestly I don't know where the patron has gone. He rushed into the office first thing this morning, gave me some money to cover expenses and said I'd have to run the place on my own for a month or even longer. He said a really big job had come up.'

'Did he tell you where?'

'No, but my guess is it could be in Russia.'

'Why Russia?'

'For a start he had his passport sticking out of his pocket and when he gave me the money he took it from an envelope that was absolutely stuffed with notes. I noticed the coat of arms of the Russian embassy on the back of the envelope, the same as the one on letters which we sometimes get.'

'He was working on a job for the Russians, wasn't he?'

The youth hesitated. 'I'm not supposed to talk about it.'

'That's all right. Fénèlon and I were colleagues when he was in the police and anyway I met him last night when he was working, at Maxim's.'

'Some job!' The youth laughed. 'It's money for nothing! All he's been doing is to follow this important Russian everywhere and see he comes to no harm. He's a wild one that Russian! The patron spends half his time paying up for damage and he takes his percentage all the time.'

'Well, when Fénèlon gets back you tell him to contact me. Immediately, or he won't be working as a detective very long.'

From Rue Gassonville, Gautier returned to the Left Bank in a mood of depression. He felt, as he had felt ever since he had been called to Impasse Louvain on the Sunday morning following the murders, that he was wasting his time in a struggle against people or forces that remained in the background, but who were more powerful than he and would have the final say.

To break the grip of this pessimism and since it was approaching the hour of the aperitif, he went to the Café Corneille. Duthrey was already there, established at their usual table with a young actor from the Comédie Française and a schoolmaster from the Lycée

Condorcet who was beginning to make a reputation as a poet. Gautier joined them and ordered himself an absinthe, which was unusual for him since he seldom drank spirits during the day.

'Taking something stronger this morning, I see,' Duthrey remarked nodding towards the absinthe. 'Are you by any chance trying to fortify yourself for the duel?'

'What duel?'

'They tell me an up and coming inspector from the Sûreté was carried away by an excess of gallantry at Maxim's last night.'

'God in Heaven!' Gautier exclaimed, mildly irritated, 'Do you journalists know everything?'

'We have men in all the best restaurants and in all the best houses too, if it comes to that, who keep us informed. We specially like to have advance warning of any duels.'

'There will be no duel.'

'A pity.' Duthrey looked at Gautier inquisitively. 'Anyway how did you come to be embroiled with the Grand Duke Varaslav?'

'It was just a misunderstanding.'

'Then that can't be the reason why he's going home.'

'What are you talking about?'

'The Russian embassy issued a statement less than an hour ago. Apparently his excellency the ambassador is being recalled to Russia suddenly—for consultations of course.'

All that afternoon Gautier sat at his desk reading and correcting a large pile of reports. The Director of the Sûreté had decided on a major review of the administration throughout the department, in order to introduce new methods and standard practices. Everything was to be controlled by regulations, from the liquid capacity of the inkwells to the form, layout and, as far as possible the language of reports. Everyone in the Sûreté except Courtrand knew it was a lunatic scheme impossible to implement in a country where every individual, every commune, every municipality believed it was their inalienable right to make their own decisions and defy conformity, in a country where only twenty years previously the Minister of Defence had discovered that army bands were playing no less than 179 different versions of the 'Marseillaise'.

Courtrand, however, refused to be diverted from the idea which he had picked up from a study of foreign police methods and for a start he had given his inspectors the task of reading through all the official reports of the last six months, editing and re-writing them as necessary so that they would fit into a new, standardized report form. Though as one man the inspectors decided that the director had gone mad, they had no choice except to obey his instructions.

As he read and annotated and edited, Gautier felt weighed down by what he recognized as a sense of remorse. The memory of the previous night, of Claudine lying naked beside him in her bed, was still sharp and sensual. He seemed almost still to feel her quick, slim body moving beneath and around his own. She had made love with a passion and aggressiveness that was almost masculine and he remembered thinking, and smiling at the thought, that it was as though she were crusading for those women's rights which she believed in so fiercely. Half-recalled sensations, the demanding pressure of her open lips on his own and the light touch of her fingers on his stomach, still played on his senses. At the same time he could not put out of his mind his return home early in the morning and the sight of Suzanne asleep in their bed. She had been sleeping contentedly, trustingly it had seemed to him and now he felt guilty for having broken that trust.

His spell of duty finished at six o'clock that day and pushing the reports thankfully to one side, he locked up his desk and went downstairs. There, to his surprise, waiting for him outside the entrance to the building was Suzanne's father. Gautier's immediate thought was a projection of his remorse; her father had come to tell him that Suzanne had been in an accident, that she was ill, that she was dead.

Instead the old man hailed him as though it were the most natural thing in the world to be waiting for his son-in-law after work. 'How goes it go, Jean-Paul?' he asked. 'Had a good day?'

'Not very. I've spent the afternoon in a futile exercise.'

'I was passing so I thought I'd walk home with you. It's a beautiful evening.'

Together they crossed the road and began walking along the Seine in the direction of the Quai d'Orsay. Monsieur Duclos was a small, rotund man whose clothes always seemed to hang on him untidily and who usually talked and laughed a good deal. Today he was unusually silent. Three or four men were fishing from the banks of the river, holding their rods out hopefully over the slowly moving water. When his father-in-law stopped and leaned on a parapet to watch one of them, Gautier did the same.

'Do you suppose they ever catch anything?' he asked the old man.

'Not now. Thirty years ago so the story goes, a man might pull out some lovely big fish. Now all the factories spew their waste into the water: tar, oil, soap, chemicals.'

'Not long ago I passed a man fishing down there and he had beside him a basket with two small fish in it.'

'Just show. He must have bought them down the road.'

Monsieur Duclos fell silent again. Gautier felt certain that he had come to meet his son-in-law for a purpose, that he had something to say and was finding it difficult to begin. Gautier wondered whether if perhaps Suzanne had somehow found out about Claudine and had sent her father to deliver a rebuke or even an ultimatum.

'I don't believe you came to the Sûreté by chance,' he said.

'What are you saying?'

'Is there something you wish to tell me?'

'Yes, you're right, Jean-Paul, but I don't know how I'm going to say it.'

Gautier smiled. 'Try the straightforward, direct way. Policemen prefer straight talk.'

'All right, then.' Monsieur Duclos looked at him miserably and Gautier thought he was going to burst into tears. 'Suzanne has found herself a lover.'

Gautier stared at him, wondering whether this was some elaborate joke, but looking away Monsieur Duclos went on, the words spilling out clumsily: 'My God, Jean-Paul, I have to tell you I'm shattered! When she told me I nearly hit her. How could she do this to you? You've always been a wonderful husband; the whole family loves and respects you and yet my daughter – yes, my favourite daughter, I have to admit it – treats you like this. She's no better than a slut, a whore.'

'Who is the man?' Gautier asked, his voice carefully controlled.

'A policeman, if you please. One of your former colleagues at the fifteenth arrondissement. He's nothing! Dirt! I feel so ashamed of Suzanne.'

'Don't be too hard on her.'

'What! You say that? After she has behaved like this?'

'I haven't exactly been innocent myself. As you probably know I had a mistress myself not long ago.'

'The girl, Monique? Yes, I knew about that, but Suzanne didn't. You had the decency to keep it from her. Anyway that was different.'

'Not really.'

'Men have mistresses. It's a fact of life. But for a well-brought-up girl of good bourgeois stock to make a cuckold of her husband! I thought it was only actresses and aristocrats who behaved like that.'

Gautier found himself wondering ironically how Claudine would have reacted to the philosophy of Monsieur Duclos. The old man had probably never even heard of women's rights.

'I left Suzanne alone too much,' he said.

'That was because of your work. Suzanne knew what to expect when she married a policeman. Don't make excuses for her.'

'Did she ask you to tell me?'

'Yes. She couldn't bring herself to do it.'

'Does that mean she wants me to move out of the apartment?'

Duclos was astounded. 'You? Move out? Jean-Paul, I came here to ask you not to thrash her, even though she richly deserves it. If you throw her out of your home no one is going to blame you.'

There was no way, Gautier began to realize, of explaining to his father-in-law how he felt. The old man was too conventional, too set in his ideas to understand why Gautier might feel guilty for having neglected his wife, whatever the reason, or why he might feel that he must take at least a share of the blame for Suzanne's infidelity.

'I don't think the girl even knows what she wants,' Duclos said angrily.

'We'll have to work it out for ourselves,' Gautier said. 'I'd better get back home.'

They walked together for a little way without speaking. There seemed to be nothing worth saying. Gautier wondered whether their relationship could ever be the same again. Duclos appeared to be humiliated by the knowledge of his daughter's behaviour and few friendships between men could survive humiliation. He would be sorry if the breach were permanent because he had always enjoyed the old man's good spirits and earthy Parisian humour.

They parted at the end of the street where Gautier lived. He went on alone and found Suzanne in the living-room of the apartment, pretending to be working at a piece of embroidery, her face drawn and tense. She looked up as he went in and then almost immediately lowered her head.

He made the only speech he could think of making. 'I'll move into the spare bedroom,' he said simply.

She began to cry, unhappy, bewildered sobs, like a small child faced unexpectedly with an adult situation which it cannot understand but which it knows intuitively will cause unhappiness. He wanted not so much to comfort her as to tell her about his own infidelity, to confess that less than 24 hours ago he had been lying naked with another woman. Then, if he could not lessen her sense of guilt, he might at least share it.

Instead he said awkwardly: 'Don't cry, chérie. You have nothing to be ashamed of.'

She reached out and touched his hand timidly. 'Jean-Paul you're so good to me. I don't deserve it,' she said between her sobs.

XVIII

THE TRIAL FOR murder of Josephine Hassler, a woman of good family but doubtful morals, the supposed mistress of a President of France, was an event which fascinated not only the whole of France, but London, New York, Moscow, Berlin, all the capitals of the civilized world. Special correspondents flooded into Paris, sending back daily accounts of the trial that ran into thousands of words. A block of seats was reserved in the court for the embassies so that ambassadors, politicians and even royalty could come to watch the spectacle. For those who had no claim to privilege, money was the only passport. One hundred seats were set aside for the public and for these the poor and the greedy queued overnight outside the Palais de Justice, selling their places next day to the highest bidder.

Although he played a negligible part in the proceedings except to give some routine evidence during the early stages, Gautier was obliged to be in court for the whole of the trial. He divided the time between trying to analyse the strategy of the prosecution and studying Josephine Hassler's performance. When she was escorted into the dock on the first day, Madame Hassler was wearing, in the face of the advice of her counsel, a black dress which, as the news-papers had already revealed, had been specially made for the occasion by one of Europe's leading couturiers, Worth. Her gestures and her expression were one of tragic martyrdom, sorrow at the great wrong that was being done her. Often she appeared crushed and pathetic, sometimes she sobbed and seemed on the point of fainting, but throughout the fourteen days of the trial, Gautier seemed to sense behind the acting and the performance a contempt for both the trappings of justice and for those who were trying her. It was as though all the time she was confident of the outcome of her trial and secure in the knowledge that she would survive it.

The Ministry of Justice had staged the spectacle well. The great Assize Court was impressive in its majesty, with the three judges in scarlet robes seated on a dais at one end and the spectators, the 100 'lucky ones' as they were called, in the public seats at the other. Between them the drama was enacted: the prisoner in the dock to the left of the judges, the jury facing her, the semi-circular witness bar in the centre beside the desks of the public prosecutor and the defence counsel and a table carrying the exhibits of the case. Near the dock was another enclosure where scores of barristers watched the trial with professional interest, looking in their black gowns and white cravats like so many carrion crows lined up and waiting for the end of the victim.

The president of the court was Judge Fourcroy and under the procedure of French criminal law, it was he in effect who conducted the trial. After the clerk of the court had read the indictment, the president examined first the prisoner and then the various witnesses. The advocate general, who was conducting the prosecution's case, and the defence counsel, Maître Bonnard, could also question the witnesses, but they had to put their questions through the president. The examination of the prisoner and witnesses would be followed by the final speeches for the prosecution and defence and the prisoner could then, if she wished, make a statement before the jury retired, without any direction or summing-up by the judge, to consider its verdict.

Gautier knew that both Judge Fourcroy and the advocate general, Rombout, were brilliant lawyers of great prestige. For this reason their appointment as president and prosecutor had been welcomed by the press and the public as proof that the government was sincere in its intention to put Josephine on trial and that there was not to be a cover-up of the scandal. Knowing the two men, he was surprised at the course which the trial took and at the tactics which the prosecution employed.

Their main objective, it seemed to him, should have been to prove that Josephine Hassler's story about the bearded robbers and the long robes was palpably untrue. This proposition should have been simple enough to demonstrate, but the advocate general handled it clumsily. He seemed to be concentrating his efforts on trying to blacken the character of the accused, always a doubtful strategy and liable, in the case of a beautiful woman to be counter-productive and win the jury's sympathy for the prisoner.

The burden of the prosecution's case was that Josephine Hassler murdered her husband in order to be free to marry a wealthy admirer who was never named; that she contrived for her mother to be present simply as a blind since people would be unlikely to believe that she would have killed her husband while her mother was in the house; that she put a sleeping tablet in her mother's grog but that this had not prevented the old lady being woken by the noise when Félix Hassler was strangled and having then had to be murdered herself; that she had explained the murders with her story modelled on an incident which she remembered from her youth.

A massive amount of evidence could have been produced to show that Josephine Hassler had lied. The prosecution, it seemed to Gautier, had selected the least convincing parts of it, introducing unsupported assertions and statements that were open to doubt if not to absolute refutation and using witnesses whom the defence were well able to confuse or discredit.

One example of this was the totally disproportionate amount of time which the prosecutor spent on the grog which Félix Hassler and his mother-in-law were supposed to have drunk on the evening of the murders. The suggestion was made that the accused had either tried unsuccessfully to poison the drinks or had put into them a sleeping draught and that she had taken the glasses down-stairs to the kitchen and washed them before staging the scene for the pretended robbery. The defence then immediately produced expert witnesses who stated that autopsies had revealed no poison or noxious substance in the bodies of the two victims.

Another clumsy attempt to prove that Josephine Hassler had lied, which also misfired, concerned the cottonwool which was supposed to have been used to gag her. Professor Bize, head of the government analytical laboratories, gave evidence that he had analysed a lump of cottonwool sent to him by the police and this had contained no traces of human saliva, which proved that it could never have been in Josephine Hassler's mouth. The counsel for the defence then pointed out that large quantities of cottonwool had been found all over the bed and on the floor of the bedroom. What proof was there, he demanded, that this particular piece of cottonwool was the one which his client had claimed to have been used to gag her? The prosecution were unable to answer the question.

The matter of the ink stain found on the sole of Hassler's foot was made into a critical issue. The family doctor who had attended Josephine Hassler on the morning after the murders, confirmed that he had noticed ink stains on the hem of her night-dress. Under questioning Madame Charon, the wife of Hassler's cousin, agreed that at Josephine's request she had taken the latter's dressing-gown to be cleaned on the day following the murders and that when handing the garment over to the cleaner, she had noticed ink stains on it.

When it was the turn of Maître Bonnard to question Madame Charon he asked her: 'You believe the ink stains on your cousin's dressing-gown were similar to those found on the body of Monsieur Hassler?'

'I cannot say. The police appear to think so.'

'And that this was ink from the ink-well which had been knocked over in the drawing-room?'

'That is what they told me.'

'We may conclude therefore that the robbers knocked over the ink-well when they were searching in the drawing-room for valuables and that some of the ink found its way on to their persons or their clothes?'

'That seems likely.'

'I agree. And if so is it not also likely that since the ink rubbed off onto Monsieur Hassler when he was being strangled, some of it might also have been expected to rub off on Madame Hassler's night attire when she was being bound and gagged?'

Maître Bonnard was allowed to score this point. To Gautier's amazement the advocate general did not intervene to point out that Josephine Hassler would not have been wearing her dressing-gown at the time when the intruders were supposed to have attacked her and that no ink stains had been found on the sheets of her bed.

The prosecution also seemed strangely half-hearted in capitalizing on the most glaring falsehoods which Josephine Hassler had told the police. Not more than a passing mention was made of the way she had falsely accused York and Claudine nor of her deliberate attempt to implicate Mansard and even her story of the duplicate rings passed almost unchallenged.

By contrast the lengths to which the prosecution went to blacken the prisoner's character were extraordinary. A stream of witnesses were produced, many of whom could have known Josephine Hassler only slightly, while others were plainly biased, society women jealous of her success with men, or artists who resented the commissions which she had obtained for her husband. When the two servants, Mansard and the cook, who might have been expected to know something about the character of their mistress, were giving evidence, the president of the court made it clear from the outset that he would not allow them to be questioned about either her character or her habits.

'I can see no reason,' he announced firmly, 'to listen to the gossip of the servants' hall.'

For fourteen days the trial continued, each session seeming longer and more futile than the last. As he listened to the questions and the arguments, Gautier would find himself thinking about Suzanne and whether she might be taking advantage of his absence to entertain her lover. He was doing all he could to make her life tolerable, to make her feel at ease, but, even more than her sense of guilt, the gratitude which she could not disguise was an insurmountable barrier between them. Whatever happened, even if she were to break with her lover and even supposing she could be convinced that he felt no jealousy or rancour, their life together could never be the same. As it was they were living from day to day, an artificial existence made up of the trivial routines of married life. What made it worse was that for some totally irrational reason he could not bring himself to see Claudine.

As he sat in the Assize Court watching Josephine Hassler, he could not help comparing Suzanne's attitude to her lapse from fidelity, probably the only sin of any consequence in her life, with that of the woman in the dock. Not once did the latter show any sign of shame or even of remorse. When she was accused of adultery she denied it imperiously in a manner which suggested not so much that she was innocent, but that she did not recognize that anything so vulgar as justice had the right to question her.

She did not, however, deny the spectators their moments of drama. From time to time she would clash with the president or the advocate general. Once when the president was losing patience with her evasive answers and high-handed manner, he instructed her to confine herself to answering his questions.

'Ah! You make your motives plain!' She turned on him accusingly. 'You don't wish me to protest my innocence! You want me to confess to these crimes because in your mind you have already tried and condemned me. Is this how you uphold justice?'

Judge Fourcroy who in Gautier's view had been more than fair to the accused was stung to rebuke her. 'Madame, you do your cause no good by this hysterical behaviour.'

'Hysterical?' She almost shouted the word at the judges. 'And why should I not be hysterical? Have you any idea how much I have suffered? Imprisoned for months with women of the streets, tortured by the examining magistrate, deprived of the company of my loved ones. Can you even conceive what this kind of treatment has done to me, a girl brought up in love and refinement? Do you not know I have been in the care of doctors who have despaired of my life?'

'Madame, for one so close to death your voice is astonishingly robust, your temper surprisingly violent.'

At last the long process of examining and re-examining more than 80 witnesses was concluded. All that remained before the jury would retire to deliberate were the speeches of the prosecution and the defence. The advocate general spoke first and his speech, lasting for almost seven hours, created a sensation, not only among the public but among the many prominent lawyers who were in court to hear it. Both his presentation of the case against Josephine Hassler and the defence of her counsel, Maître Bonnard, were later included in the series *Great Criminal Trials of France*, standard reading for all law students.

The advocate general, Rombout, besides his great intellect and powers of oratory, was known as a calm, unemotional man who won convictions with the deadly logic and simplicity of his arguments. Maître Bonnard, on the other hand, was a brilliant pleader who by his eloquent persuasion had often led juries into shutting their eyes to damning evidence.

In the trial of the Impasse Louvain murders, their usual rôles were reversed. Rombout constructed his speech around an attack on the prisoner which in its bitterness and contempt surpassed anything that had been heard in the courts of France for many years. He began by speaking of Josephine's childhood, describing how her wilful and selfish behaviour had turned her father into a drunkard and made life unbearable for the rest of the family. Her engagement to the young army officer had, he claimed, been broken off not by her parents but by his, when they had learnt about her scandalous behaviour. He went on to assert that Josephine had only married Félix Hassler to get to Paris where she could lead a life of depravity, that she had turned her sister-in-law out of her husband's house, that she had bullied her servants, that she had shamelessly used her body to advance her ambitions.

'You see this woman before you,' Rombout said to the jury pointing at the accused. 'A courtesan who entertained men in her husband's very home, who took lavish presents for the charms she bestowed so freely, who lied and cheated and schemed so that she could live a life of pleasure and luxury, who accepted the devotion of a husband all the time she was deceiving him, who, when she saw the prize she had always coveted within her grasp, had no hesitation in murdering this devoted husband so she would be free to marry into wealth and power.'

Turning to the murders at Impasse Louvain, the advocate general denounced Josephine Hassler's story as a tissue of lies, but he did not, as one would have expected, go over the story, exposing the contradictions and inconsistencies to destroy it step by step. Instead he explained that Madame Hassler was being accused only of her husband's murder and that the prosecution believed that her mother's death had been accidental. Madame Pinock, he said, had been brought to the house as part of the murder plan. She was to be attacked and tied up by the accomplices of the accused so that she would be able to confirm that intruders had broken into the house, which would lead the police to assume that it was these intruders who had killed Monsieur Hassler. In fact, even as the old lady was being attacked, Josephine Hassler was strangling her husband. Then Madame Pinock had upset the plan by swallowing her dentures and choking to death.

This argument was the first admission by the prosecution that the murders could not have been the work of Josephine Hassler alone. Up to that point the possibility of her having accomplices had scarcely been mentioned throughout the trial. Now, having introduced the subject, the advocate general went on to make an extraordinary allegation.

'We know that one of the accomplices,' he stated, 'was a relative of one of the accused woman's servants. Unfortunately we do not have enough evidence yet to put that person on trial.'

There could be no doubt about whom he was accusing. Pierre Malin, the son of the Hassler's cook Françoise, had been interrogated more than once by the police and by the examining magistrate, and some newspapers had hinted openly that he was one of the suspects. For the advocate general to make such an accusation in his closing speech was unprecedented, a radical departure from French legal practise. It drew murmurs of surprise from all the lawyers in court and a dramatic reaction from Maître Bonnard.

The defence counsel leapt to his feet. 'The prosecutor speaks of knowing the names of accomplices. I know that as a man of honour he will not refuse to answer this question—Is he naming Pierre Malin, the son of my client's cook?'

Instead of replying, Rombout drew his gown more closely around himself and turning to the jury continued his speech. He said: 'There is no law in France which says that this woman cannot be tried alone and without her accomplices. You the jury have seen her in the dock. You have seen her behaviour: proud, insolent and totally without remorse. She has spoken of her husband and her mother with equanimity and composure and without showing any signs of the grief one would expect from an innocent woman. You have no alternative, members of the jury, but to find her guilty and for a crime so heinous and so depraved the law can only demand the maximum penalty, the guillotine.'

In following this speech, Maître Bonnard had, it seemed to Gautier, a simple task. Piece by piece he demolished the case of the prosecution, reminding the jury repeatedly that nothing but circumstantial evidence had been produced against his client. He explained the inconsistencies in her statements and her attempt to incriminate others by reminding the jury of the dreadful experience she had suffered, of the strain to which she had been exposed, of her interrogation by the police and of the way she had been pestered by journalists.

'Indeed, you may think,' Maître Bonnard added, 'that these small slips, these lapses of memory are a sure proof of Madame Hassler's innocence. A guilty woman, surely, would have had her story ready and stuck to it without ever changing a single word.'

He pointed out how even during the trial the prosecution had shifted its ground on the question of possible accomplices. With heavy irony he mocked the attempt to produce scientific experts who would bolster up a weak case and poured scorn on the confusion of these experts and the failure of the prosecution to make anything of their allegations about the drugged grog, the ink stains and the cottonwool gags.

Finally Maître Bonnard moved into an eloquent and impassioned plea for Josephine Hassler. Angrily he denounced the attempts of the prosecution to blacken her character. He told the jury of her devotion to her husband and her daughter, her good works, her gifts to the poor. Here was a woman, he told them, into whose house eminent people had been glad to go with their wives. Were the jury being asked to believe that such people would have consorted with an adulteress and a murderer?

'The prosecution has sought to condemn this woman for her bearing in court, for the courage and determination with which she has denied the monstrous accusation of a repugnant and unnatural crime. She has fought, yes and why not? She is fighting for her life, members of the jury and that is all she has left. Her happiness and that of her loving daughter have already been destroyed not once but twice: once by the foul murderers who killed a devoted and beloved husband and father; once by the police, the newspapers and the public with their slanders, their accusations and their calumny. Josephine Hassler fights with dignity for her life and her freedom and I am confident that you, members of the jury, will in the name of justice, knowing her to be falsely accused, give her both.'

138

It was just before one o'clock on a Friday when the jury retired. With nothing left to do but wait for the verdict, Gautier left the court and went to the Café Corneille which, as he had expected, he found crowded with lawyers and journalists who had been at the trial. Everyone was talking about the unusual way in which the advocate general had handled the case for the prosecution. Duthrey was among them and he spoke cynically about the motives of the authorities.

'We forced them to put her on trial,' he declared, 'but the government didn't want her found guilty. An acquittal is to be her reward for keeping silent over the late president.'

'It was all a cover-up,' a young lawyer suggested. 'One can't believe that the cook's son was the Hassler woman's accomplice. If you ask me someone much more important is being shielded.'

'She'll be found guilty,' another lawyer put in, 'the jury won't be deceived by Rombout's tactics.

On Duthrey's suggestion they decided to hold a poll among themselves on what the verdict should be and as it happened there were twelve men sitting at the table. Duthrey tore up some paper into voting slips which he passed round the group.

'Are we supposed to vote on whether we think she is guilty?' Gautier asked.

'Good God, no! We all know she's guilty. Just write down how you think the jury will vote.'

Everyone in the group wrote on his slip of paper, folded it and handed it to Duthrey who had appointed himself, as he said, foreman of the jury. While he was counting the votes some of the journalists began to bet on the result.

'By ten votes to two,' Duthrey announced after he had counted the slips, 'Madame Hassler is acquitted.'

To fill in the time until the real jury returned, the whole group went and lunched at the Cloiserie des Lilas, a restaurant which had made its name as a meeting place for poets and artists. The lunch was long and leisurely and alcoholic. Under the mellowing influence of red wine, Gautier found his irritation at the way Josephine Hassler's trial had been conducted gradually disappearing. Although he was certain she had been involved in her husband's murder, he was almost prepared to concede that it was less than fair that she should stand trial alone, while the person who had actually strangled Hassler remained free.

They were all back in court when, at twenty-past-five the jury returned. Before the verdict was formally announced another inspector from the Sûreté, who had been waiting outside the jury room, slipped into the seat next to Gautier.

'It's not guilty,' he said.

'I was sure it would be,' Gautier replied.

'It was touch and go. The vote was only seven to five and it seems that when they took the first count it was eight to four for guilty. But then some of the ones who thought she should be acquitted talked the others round.'

The announcement of the verdict, although it came as an anti-climax to Gautier, created a sensation in the court. A brief silence was quickly shattered first by a burst of cheering, then by much louder counter cheers and booing. Maître Bonnard and his assistants came forward to congratulate Josephine Hassler and then hurried her out of court. Before she left she stopped by the door of the court for a moment and turned to look at those who had tried her and those who had watched her trial. There was no relief and no pleasure in her expression, no gratitude nor emotion, only a defiant contempt.

Outside the court Gautier met Courtrand who had managed to procure himself one of the very few seats reserved at the trial for important people. Courtrand said to him: 'The right verdict, I think.'

'Does that mean you don't believe she was guilty?' Gautier asked him bluntly.

'My dear Inspector,' Courtrand's tone held no more than the merest hint of sarcasm. 'All I believe is that we didn't put a very good case into court.'

XIX

ONE MORNING DURING the week following the end of the trial, Surat came into Gautier's office. He had the apologetic air of a man who came with news that might be unwelcome.

'Is the Impasse Louvain affair still of any interest, patron?' he enquired diffidently.

'Officially we have been told that the case is closed, but that doesn't mean it might not be re-opened. Why?'

'For some weeks now I've been keeping an eye on the coachman from the Russian embassy. He's very careful, that one, or he has been well paid to keep his mouth shut. But last night at last I managed to fill him up with a lot of Calvados and his tongue began to wag.'

'What did you learn?'

'That the Grand Duke Varaslav was at the Hasslers' house on the night of the murders. The coachman dropped him off at the entrance to the street with another man, a detective whom the embassy had employed to accompany the ambassador everywhere.'

'Yes, I know who that would be.'

'But if the grand duke was implicated in the murders then one or two things will have to be explained.'

'Such as?'

'For example he evidently appears to have left the house well before the time when the murders are supposed to have been committed. The coachman swears he dropped the grand duke at Impasse Louvain not much after ten at the latest, and that he stayed only a short time, perhaps half-an-hour.'

'That could be just long enough.'

'To murder Hassler, tie him and the old lady up, fix the rooms so they would seem to have been ransacked by thieves?'

'Yes, if it had been carefully planned in advance.'

'Ah, there we have another snag.'

Surat explained that although the grand duke had arranged to see Josephine Hassler that evening, he had called at her house much earlier than he had intended. The coachman had taken the grand duke together with his wife and daughter to a special charity performance at the Opera and he had been instructed that at the conclusion of the performance he was to take the ambassador to Impasse Louvain, while another coach would take the grand duchess and her daughter to a reception to be held by the Ministry of Fine Arts who had organized the performance at the Opera. During the interval of the performance however, the coachman had been summoned by the detective Fénèlon and had taken both men to Impasse Louvain.

'The coachman seems to believe that the Grand Duke Varaslav was drunk and that he had quarrelled with his wife.'

'He seems a talkative philosopher, this coachman,' Gautier remarked. 'Did he have any ideas on why the ambassador stayed such a short time at the Hasslers' house?'

'He wasn't surprised at that. Apparently the grand duke never wasted much time with his women. Easily aroused and quickly satisfied, so the coachman said.'

'So he's saying his master left the house soon after half-past-ten?'

'Yes, that's about it.'

Gautier got up from his desk, crossed the room and stared thoughtfully out of the window. Rain was being slanted across the city by a cold breeze from the north-east. An old woman on the far side of the street was holding her arm bent across her forehead as protection and leaning into the wind as she walked. Two fiacres were stationed waiting for custom on the corner of the street, the drivers sheltering inside the carriages while the horses stood dumb and uncomplaining in the driving rain.

What Surat had just told him had blocked off yet another of the paths which his mind had been exploring in an effort to arrive at the truth about the Impasse Louvain affair. Now it seemed clear that the Grand Duke Varaslav could not have been implicated in the murders. The fact that he had been packed off back to Russia and the detective Fénèlon bribed to leave Paris proved nothing.

Even if the ambassador was innocent the Russian government, knowing he had visited the Hassler household that night, would have wished to get him out of France to avoid any chance of his name being dragged into the scandal.

At the same time Gautier had a very strong presentiment that he was now not far from learning the truth. There must be one factor, itself probably unimportant, which he had overlooked or misunderstood and which would provide the key to open the final door.

As he stood by the window thinking, his stare became focused on a distant church clock on the other side of the Seine. Its hands stood at half-past-eleven. For almost a minute he looked at it, aware of an unformed idea which nagged at his conscious mind, telling him that the position of the hands, the time they showed, were in some undefined way significant.

Then he remembered. Half-past-eleven was the time at which the alarm clock by the side of Félix Hassler's bed had been set. Immediately from this starting point, his mind leapt forward moving from idea to idea at breathless speed. Suddenly he was left with a theory which, improbable though it might appear, provided the only logical answer to a dozen questions.

'Come on,' he called to Surat as he crossed towards the door of the office.

'Where are we going?'

'To the Ritz Hotel.'

Their visit to the Ritz was brief. They were received in an office near the reception desk by an assistant manager whose impeccable morning coat was matched only by his impeccable manners. When Gautier explained that he wished to speak with the doorman who had been on duty at the hotel's Rue Cambon entrance on the night of 31 May, the assistant manager went to great trouble, checking through a mass of staff records and duty sheets which had been filed away.

'We are not often required to check these records,' he explained with an apologetic smile and then when he had found the sheets he needed he added: 'Ah, I feared as much, Inspector. It is Vallière whom you will wish to see.'

'And is that not possible?'

'Vallière has left our service; more than a month ago.'

Gautier looked at the assistant manager, sensing a hint of disapproval in the man's tone. 'And may I ask why?'

'He was dismissed for dishonesty. The hotel decided not to lay any charges against him, of course. The scoundrel was probably counting on that.'

The assistant manager was not able to say whether the doorman had found another post or where he was living, but that information did not take long to unearth. Surat was allowed into the hotel kitchens to speak with members of the staff and he soon returned with the answers. Vallière, it seemed, had bought a hotel of his own in Rue St Denis.

As he and Gautier were leaving the Ritz, Surat remarked: 'This Vallière must have swindled on a big scale to have made enough to buy a hotel.'

'Not necessarily. Guests at these top-class places tip well. The doorman at Maxim's bought himself a château in the Pyrénées when he retired.'

Surat sighed. 'Who'd be a policeman!'

Vallière's place in Rue St Denis, the Hotel de Soleil, proved to be an establishment very different from the Ritz. Its tiny entrance was squeezed between two shops and on the three floors above there were perhaps six to eight bedrooms. Even without the sign posted on the door 'Chambres à Louer' one would have instantly recognized the place for what it was—a hotel de rendez-vous to which the streetwalkers in the district took their clients. There were hundreds of similar hotels to be found in Paris, around the railway stations, near the Moulin Rouge and the big Café Concerts, in Pigalle and on the Left Bank.

They found Vallière behind a small reception desk in the narrow lobby of the hotel. He was a tall, slim man in his late thirties who would have been good-looking but for his small, mean eyes.

Wasting no time on preliminaries, Gautier identified himself to Vallière and then said: 'We're making enquiries about a matter which took place when you were working at the Ritz.'

'Hey, wait a minute! The hotel isn't pressing charges.'

'You misunderstand me. We've not come about anything you did.'

'Then what?'

'We're interested in a certain Colonel de Clermont who's a regular patron of the Ritz. You know who I mean of course.'

'Hundreds of colonels stay there,' Vallière replied evasively. 'It's that sort of place.'

'You know the man all right. He had a lady friend who visited him in his suite and always used the Rue Cambon entrance. No doubt you looked after the lady from time to time; called up a fiacre for her and so on and no doubt the colonel was suitably grateful.'

'I don't remember.'

Gautier was beginning to lose patience with the man and his voice took on a much harsher tone as he said:

'Then let us see whether we can revive your memory. If not I'll arrange that from this afternoon a policeman will patrol the pavement outside your hotel 24 hours a day.'

'You can't do that. What girl is going to bring a man here if there's a flic hanging around?'

'Precisely.'

After a short, surly silence Vallière shrugged his shoulders. 'All right, have it your way. Yes, I remember the colonel. He was a real gentleman who knew how to behave. Once or twice I was able to do him a small favour and he always showed his appreciation.'

'Right. Now I want you to cast your mind back to the night of Saturday 31 May. You were on duty that night at the Rue Cambon entrance of the hotel.'

'My God, that was months ago! How can I be expected to remember that far back.'

'It was a special night for the colonel. He had come to Paris to attend the dinner of the Cercle Agricole. He went to the dinner and returned to the hotel soon after eleven o'clock and took his key from the night porter. We have reason to believe that he then walked through the hotel to the Rue Cambon entrance and went out again. No doubt you fetched him a fiacre.'

'Well, he went out late at night more than once, I can tell you.'

'I'm sure he did, but this was also a special night for another gentleman, a Monsieur Félix Hassler. He was murdered that night.'

'Mother of God! The Impasse Louvain murders! You're surely not trying to say the colonel was involved.'

'The lady whom Colonel de Clermont invited up to his suite so often was Madame Hassler.'

Vallière stared at Gautier in dumb astonishment. Behind the stare his mind was working laboriously assembling the implications of what he had just been told. Though he was quick enough in calculating ten per cent or when it came to pocketing a tip, reasoning was not Vallière's most conspicuous talent.

'My God!' he exclaimed again and then laughed. 'The cunning bastard! And to think I never put two and two together! If I had, it would have cost him a lot more than a ten-franc tip, I can tell you!'

'Come on, let's have the full story.'

Now that his memory had been stimulated, it was remarkable how clearly Vallière remembered the events of the night of 31 May. Colonel de Clermont, as Gautier guessed, had indeed gone out again after returning from his club dinner. Vallière had whistled up a fiacre for him from the corner of Rue Cambon and he even remembered the driver of the fiacre, a solid dependable fellow whom he had often arranged to hire when the job was a delicate one and the pay likely to be good, for they had an 'arrangement'. The colonel had been well on the way to being drunk, Vallière had noticed, and he had muttered about wanting to go and see a lady on the Left Bank. He had returned to the hotel in the same fiacre at about one-thirty a good deal more sober. Vallière also remembered that his shirt front was badly stained with what looked like ink.

'He gave me ten francs and said I was to be sure not to tell anyone about his little late-night adventure.' Vallière concluded. 'I took it for granted he'd been to some high-class whore shop.'

'You may be required to make a statement on oath later,' Gautier told the man as he and Surat prepared to leave the Hotel de Soleil. 'You've been very helpful.'

'Not willingly. Remember that! It's a fine thing when the police stoop to blackmail.'

XX

A PERSISTENT DRIZZLE, almost too fine and too light to deserve the name of rain, hung over the featureless countryside as Gautier was being driven from the railway station to the Château d'Ivry. This was typical autumn weather, he reflected. He had never understood how people found romance in autumn; to him it was a season of damp and decay, of sadness for the spent virility of summer and forlorn expectation of a cheerless winter. The Château d'Ivry itself, shrouded in the drizzle, seemed silent and unresponsive, as though immersed in gloomy thoughts of its own.

The manservant who opened the door to him was the same one as on his previous visit and he was kept waiting in the hall, while the man went to see whether his master would consent to see Gautier. A full-length portrait of a large woman with thick lips and a swollen bosom, presumably the colonel's late wife, hung on the wall facing the front door. The expression on the face of the woman was a combination of greed and disappointment, as though in her life she had lusted for many things, material possessions, fine clothes, men and had found them all without ever finding satisfaction.

In a few moments the servant returned and ushered Gautier into the study where Colonel de Clermont, dressed in riding habit, was standing looking out of the window. The setting, the colonel's stance and posture, the position of the books and papers which lay on his desk were so similar to everything he remembered from his last visit that Gautier could not help feeling that he was looking at a photograph.

'I can't imagine what business brings you here, Inspector,' de Clermont said without looking round. 'I read in the papers that Madame Hassler's trial had ended and that she had been acquitted.'

'That's true, but the case has not been closed. It cannot be closed until the person who killed Félix Hassler has been brought to trial and convicted.'

'You speak almost as though you knew who killed the man.' De Clermont turned round to look at Gautier. His mouth was smiling but his eyes were watchful.

'Oh I do, Colonel. I do.'

'Really? Or are you guessing once again? Just as you guessed that Josephine must have strangled her husband and gagged and bound herself to her bed?'

'We were right about one thing. Madame Hassler was lying. And you were lying, Colonel, when you said you had not been at Impasse Louvain that day. You went to the Hasslers' house after you returned from your club dinner.'

De Clermont made a contemptuous noise. 'Are you suggesting that I conspired with Josephine to kill her husband?'

'No. I believe you had no intention of going to see your mistress that evening. Probably you had a rendez-vous for lunch the following day. But when you got back to the Ritz from your club dinner, full of drink no doubt, your infatuation – or your lust – was too strong and on a sudden whim you jumped into a fiacre and went to her house.'

'You can prove all this of course?' The colonel's tone was still self-assured and mocking.

'I think so. The doorman at the Ritz has made a statement and we've found the fiacre driver who took you to Impasse Louvain and whom you kept waiting for more than an hour.'

'Even supposing I did go round to see Josephine, why should I have killed her husband and her mother?'

'I'm quite sure you didn't go there with the intention of killing anyone.'

'Then I repeat, why should I have killed Hassler?'

'Because of your violent temper. The same temper which has caused you trouble in the past; which led you to attack a fellow officer in the army so savagely that you were compelled to resign your commission. We've been checking on your past, Colonel.' A shadow of discontent passed over de Clermont's face, as though the memory of his resignation from the army still rankled as an injustice. Gautier went on: 'You were unlucky that night at Impasse

148

Louvain. At any other time Josephine Hassler would probably have welcomed you and her husband would certainly never have disturbed your love-making. But they had arranged a little trap for one of her other lovers that night, you see, and by sheer bad luck the trap was sprung on you.'

'A trap? Another lover? What on earth are you talking about?'

'I imagine that the scene was set for something like this. The Grand Duke Varaslav had arranged to call on Josephine after going to the Opera. Her mother had been put to bed with a sleeping draught and her husband was in his room waiting. Hassler was a man who dropped off to sleep easily so he had set his alarm clock to wake him in case that happened. The scheme was that he was to go down to the drawing-room and confront the grand duke in flagrante as it were. The grand duke wouldn't like a scandal, so the poor husband would have to be compensated for his injured feelings. It isn't a very original plot. I imagine they would be asking for a few hundred thousand francs; just the amount they needed to pay off their debts. That wouldn't be much to a man of the grand duke's wealth.'

'Are you saying that Josephine Hassler would stoop to blackmail?'

'She was desperate. I daresay she was trying to raise money from all her friends. Perhaps she asked you for some.' Gautier could see from de Clermont's expression that he had guessed correctly. He continued: 'Unfortunately the grand duke, like you, grew impatient. He left the Opera at the interval and went to Impasse Louvain much earlier than Josephine had expected. She probably tried to persuade him to prolong his stay until eleven-thirty, the time when Félix would be making his entrance, but the grand duke was not that sort of lover. Once his craving had been satisfied he lurched off into the night and as for Félix Hassler, he actually had fallen asleep. Then soon afterwards you arrived. I don't suppose it ever crossed Josephine's mind to warn her husband. The plot to fleece the grand duke had misfired so there was no reason to turn you away. She may have thought that even if he did disturb the two of you by mistake, he could easily have been packed off back to bed. But when he did appear at the door in his night shirt you lost your temper. You may have even thought that

149

you were going to be blackmailed or perhaps it was just injured vanity at being caught in the classic, undignified position. So you grabbed Félix by the throat and strangled him. You may have only wished to frighten him but in your drunken rage you were carried away.'

Colonel de Clermont stared at Gautier, obviously shaken. Gautier wondered whether in his mind he was living the horror of that drunken scene in the Hasslers' house and recalling the numbing realization that he had killed a man.

'Josephine Hassler remained calm,' Gautier said. 'It must have been she who conceived the plan to set a scene which would look as though the house had been burgled and her husband killed when the intruders attacked him. You carried the body upstairs to Hassler's bedroom. But when you began to tie up the old lady, she woke up so you stuffed cottonwool into her mouth to stop her screaming. You were not to know that she would swallow her false teeth and choke herself. Finally to complete the deception you tied Josephine Hassler to her bed and then just walked out of the house. It was all so simple: no witnesses, very little noise and no evidence to show that you had even been there that night.'

'Exactly!' De Clermont said quickly. 'No evidence. Let us pretend for a moment that what you've said is true. Can you prove any of it?'

'As I've told you, we have found the fiacre driver who took you to Impasse Louvain.'

'What does that prove? I called on a lady friend. When I left she and her husband were both alive and well.'

'The doorman of the Ritz will testify that your shirt was stained with ink.'

'So he accuses me now, months after the murders and after he has read all about the trial in the papers and about the ink stains. Why didn't he come forward before? And who is going to believe him anyway, a man dismissed from his job for dishonesty?' De Clermont had regained both his composure and his arrogance. 'And will you bring Madame Hassler into court again, Inspector, to accuse her if not of murder then of conspiracy. No, I think we can be sure that after one failure your superiors will never allow your case to go to trial.'

Gautier knew the man was right. The evidence he could produce was not enough to force the hand of those members of the government who had been reluctant in the first place to put Josephine Hassler on trial and who must have been relieved when she had been acquitted. He had made the trip from Paris to the Château d'Ivry with a vague, undefined hope that a confrontation with Colonel de Clermont might produce, if not a confession then some admission which could be turned into evidence. Realizing now that he could gain nothing by prolonging the interview, he turned towards the door.

'We shall see about that, Colonel,' he said, and left the room.

As he crossed the hallway towards the front door, he noticed that as on his previous visit, the door to the drawing-room was slightly open and the same faded woman stood watching from the room beyond. As he came up level with the door, she opened it wider and beckoned him.

'Do you want me?' he asked enquiringly.

The woman placed a finger on her lips to silence him, reached out to catch the sleeve of his coat and pulled him towards the open door. He followed her into the drawing-room.

'What is it?' Gautier asked.

She had the crushed, nervous look of an animal or small child that has been persistently ill-treated. Apart from that and the premature lines of age in her face, she could have been pretty. Her clothes were drab and colourless and her hands, he noticed, were coarsened by work.

With a furtive, secretive air she crossed the room and produced from behind a settee where it had been hidden, a cloth bag. Bringing it to Gautier she opened the bag and pulled out a man's crumpled dress shirt.

'Look!' She smiled maliciously.

Gautier took the rolled up shirt and shook it out. Its starched front and both of the cuffs were liberally stained with what looked like ink.

'He brought it back from Paris on the day after that woman's husband was murdered,' the woman said.

'Are you certain?'

'Oh yes. He unpacked his own suitcase after coming back from

Paris that time, which made me suspicious. So I checked his linen and found that one of his dress shirts was missing. That same evening I watched from my bedroom and saw him go out and hide something in a pile of rubbish that was to be burned the following morning. I waited until it was dark and then went out to see what it was and I found this shirt.' She looked at Gautier anxiously. 'That will be enough evidence won't it? I mean your scientists will be able to prove it was the same ink.'

'Why did you keep the shirt?' Gautier asked her. 'You would not even have heard of the murders at the time.'

'If he went to so much trouble to destroy it, then I guessed it might be connected with something discreditable. So I hid it just in case I might one day be able to use it to harm him. Then when I read in the papers about that Hassler woman's trial, I knew he must have been involved.'

'Why didn't you go to the police as soon as you knew?'

'He would have been suspicious if I had tried to leave the house. I never go out except to church on Sundays. So I just waited, knowing you'd come back.'

Gautier folded the shirt carefully and began putting it back into the cloth bag. The woman watched him and he found himself wondering at the depth of her hatred for her step-father.

'Will that be proof enough?' she asked him again.

'I would think so, added to the other evidence which we have to show that he was at the murdered man's house.'

'He has to be destroyed,' the woman said slowly. 'All his life he has used other people, dominated them, destroyed them. Now it's his turn. It's God's justice.'

Gautier was standing with his back to the drawing-room door as he put the shirt away and suddenly he noticed a look of terror in the woman's eyes as she looked past him. He spun round in time to see the door, which had been slightly ajar, closing quietly.

'My God!' the woman shouted. 'It was him. He heard everything!'

Leaping across the room Gautier pulled the door open and ran into the hall, getting there just in time to see de Clermont disappear into the study and slam that door behind him. He followed with the colonel's step-daughter close behind him, but when they burst into the study the room was empty.

'There!' The woman pointed towards a door at the far end of the study which, since the windows were all closed, could have been the only way by which the colonel could have left the room.

'Where does it lead?'

'Only to the gun room.'

When they reached the door it was locked. Gautier lifted up his fist to hammer on it; before he had time to strike a single blow, a deafening report came from the room beyond, followed by a sound that could have been made by a body falling.

The colonel's step-daughter screamed. After a few seconds a little blood trickled under the door and across the floor of the study.

XXI

GAUTIER DID NOT return to Paris until the following afternoon. The suicide of Colonel de Clermont had meant much for him to do. He had sent for a doctor, called the police, informed the local authorities. His statement and that of the colonel's step-daughter had been taken and formally attested. So he had stayed overnight in the village of Toussaint and caught the mid-day train to Paris.

In his office at the Sûreté, he finished writing the report which he had started the previous evening at Toussaint and on which he had worked during the train journey. It was a concise account of all the information he had assembled which together showed that de Clermont had been involved in the Impasse Louvain affair, the statements he had taken from the former doorman of the Ritz, the fiacre coachman and the colonel's step-daughter and finally the vital evidence of the ink-stained evening dress shirt.

When the report was finished, he took it in to Courtrand. He had sent the director a long telegraph the previous afternoon in which he had set out the circumstances of de Clermont's suicide, so the report he knew would not come as a total surprise. Even so he fully expected to be greeted with a burst of anger because not only had he disobeyed Courtrand's orders but he had proved him wrong.

Instead to his surprise Courtrand received him courteously. 'You've finished your report already? Excellent! And I can see that it's as comprehensive and precise as usual.' After flicking through the report Courtrand added: 'You're to be commended, Gautier, for the way you have solved this difficult crime and salvaged the reputation of the department.'

Gautier found it difficult to conceal his astonishment. There seemed to be no limits to Courtrand's flair for the unexpected. All he could do was ask: 'And what happens now?'

'Ah yes, what indeed! That's a problem which has been exercising my mind ever since we received your telegram. And not only my mind. The minister and even more important personages have had to be consulted. The suicide of this Colonel de Clermont stops us from bringing him to justice.'

'And Madame Hassler?'

'She has already left France for London where, they say, she will shortly be marrying an English milord. Madame Hassler is indeed a problem. If we attempted to bring her back and made fresh charges, there would be a public outcry. She won a lot of sympathy for herself at the trial.'

'I can see there would be legal difficulties in putting her on trial alone,' Gautier remarked.

'Precisely. So there will be no trial.'

'At least we can issue a full statement of what has happened to the press.'

'That's exactly what I would have liked to do,' Courtrand said, 'but I have been instructed that there can be no statement.'

Gautier was astounded. 'In that event no one will ever know that the case was solved!'

'The matter has been taken out of my hands, Gautier. I can tell you in confidence that no less a personage that the president himself has decided that no useful purpose would be served by issuing a statement. The case is to be officially and finally closed, the dossier filed away.'

'But that's unfair!' Gautier protested. 'Unfair on all the people who have worked on the case and unfair on the reputation of the department.'

Courtrand opened his two hands in a gesture of helplessness. ' I agree with you entirely. I was very angry about it. But sometimes the public good dictates that we cannot say all we know, even if it means that the world at large thinks we have failed. It's something which we as servants of the State must learn to endure.'

Gautier knew there was nothing to be gained by arguing. What Courtrand had said was in principle true, although he suspected that the decision to close the case might have been made not by the president but by Courtrand himself. To publish the facts of the case would be to admit that the rash public statement which

Courtrand had made in the early days of the case denying that Josephine Hassler could in any way be implicated in the murders, had been wrong. A man of his vanity would not easily make such an admission.

The interview was over but as Gautier made to leave the room, Courtrand remarked: 'You've done yourself a lot of good by the way you handled this case, Gautier. It's been noted in the highest places.' He smiled as he added: 'And, of course some of the credit will fall on me; for picking you as exactly the right man to put in charge.'

Walking back home from the Sûreté, Gautier felt a sense of relief as the frustration which had been building up inside him almost since that first Sunday when he had been called to Impasse Louvain, ebbed away. The fact that the case was to be closed without the truth ever being made known did not irritate him as much as he expected. He had the personal satisfaction of knowing that the crime had been solved, the ends tied up, and that was enough.

For a few days or with any luck even weeks, he would have time to live his own life and disentangle his own problems. He told himself that he would have to do something about Suzanne. He felt no anger, no jealousy for what she had done, only pity for the misery which her sense of guilt was causing her. Even so the situation that had been created was impossible to live with and he accepted that it was he who must take the initiative and change it.

A vague plan was forming in his mind. Part of Suzanne's feelings for him may have been atrophied by the familiarity of marriage and by his neglect of her, but something must remain which could be aroused. Words would be useless and he must show her by his actions that he still had need, if not of a passionate love, then of her affection and companionship. He might make a start that very night, insist that she go out to dine with him and afterwards they could drop in at her parents' home. Suzanne might need persuading but if there were even a trace of her affection left for him, that should not be difficult.

When he let himself into their apartment and found it in darkness, he knew intuitively that his good resolutions had come too late. Suzanne had left a note for him, propped up against the clock that had been a wedding present from her god-father. The note read:

Chéri,
I cannot bear to stay on watching you suffer and knowing what I have done to you. So I am leaving, but not to go and live with him. I have taken only my clothes because everything else belongs to the husband.
Forgive me,

Suzanne.
P.S. All your linen has been washed and ironed.

Gautier crumpled the note and threw it into the empty fireplace. Then looking for something to drink and finding only a bottle of Calvados, he poured himself a glass of it and sat down to think. Another man might have rushed after his wife, gone to her parents' home, demanded his rights, but that was not his style. Either Suzanne would return of her own accord, beg his forgiveness and they would be reconciled, or the marriage had crumbled and fallen apart irretrievably. His mood was one of fatalism.

The only problem was the present. The prospect of spending the evening alone in the apartment, with or without the solace of drink, called for a greater effort of will than he was able to make. Some inner force, a compound of pride and remorse and stubbornness, prevented him from going to Claudine. It was too late in the evening to look for the companionship of friends at the Café Corneille; by this time they would be at home with their wives.

Drearily he began in his mind to plan his evening: a lonely aperitif in some café on the Boulevard St Germain; a meal in a modest restaurant; a couple of beers in some place where there would be music, a caf'conc perhaps, with its vulgarity and laughter; afterwards if he was drunk enough to forget discrimination, he might stumble off to a hotel de rendez-vous with one of the many girls that all these places offered.

Wearily he swallowed what remained of the Calvados, got up and went into the kitchen to rinse out his glass. Domestic chores, he reflected, were going to add a new responsibility to his daily routine and one which required discipline. By an illogical association of ideas, the thought brought to his mind a picture of Claudine, wiping her paint-brushes on an old rag and with the thought came a sharp stab of longing, partly desire, partly a longing for company and sympathy.

He was cursing himself mildly when he heard knocking on the door. It must be Suzanne, he decided, or her father with apologies and offers of reconciliation. The prospect filled him with despondency. Resignedly he opened the door. Outside stood a policeman, the same man from the fifteenth arrondissement who had been sent months ago to summon him to Impasse Louvain.

'What is it?' Gautier asked.

'A message from the Sûreté, Monsieur l'Inspecteur. The body of a young woman has been found in the house of the Minister of the Interior. The director has instructed that you are to go and take charge of the investigations.'